THEY CAME TO VIRGINIA CITY

Gwen Quinn—Her father's mine would go bankrupt if she couldn't get through with her supplies. She could not let herself be delayed, not by Indians, and certainly not by falling in love.

Grant Jordan—He had drifting in his blood until he saved Gwen as the lone survivor of an Indian ambush. Now he was caught up in her dangerous mission—and it could cost him his life.

Captain William Rutledge—A bitter, ambitious officer, he would teach the hostiles a lesson, even if it meant a bloody massacre.

Jess Clum—As the most influential man in the territory even the army would listen to him, and he was the sworn enemy of Gwen and her father.

The Stagecoach Series
Ask your bookseller for the books you have missed

STAGECOACH STATION 5:

VIRGINIA CITY

Hank Mitchum

Created by the producers of
**Wagons West, White Indian,
Saga of the Southwest,** and
The Kent Family Chronicles Series.

Executive Producer: Lyle Kenyon Engel

BANTAM BOOKS
TORONTO · NEW YORK · LONDON · SYDNEY

STAGECOACH STATION 5: VIRGINIA CITY

*A Bantam Book / published by arrangement with
Book Creations, Inc.*

Bantam edition / April 1983

*Produced by Book Creations, Inc.
Executive Producer: Lyle Kenyon Engel.*

ISBN 0-553-23144-8

Published simultaneously in the United States and Canada

Bantam Books are published by Bantam Books, Inc. Its trademark,
consisting of the words ''Bantam Books'' and the portrayal of a
rooster, is Registered in U.S. Patent and Trademark Office and in
other countries. Marca Registrada. Bantam Books, Inc., 666 Fifth
Avenue, New York, New York 10103.

PRINTED IN THE UNITED STATES OF AMERICA

O   0 9 8 7 6 5 4 3 2 1

STAGECOACH STATION 5:

VIRGINIA CITY

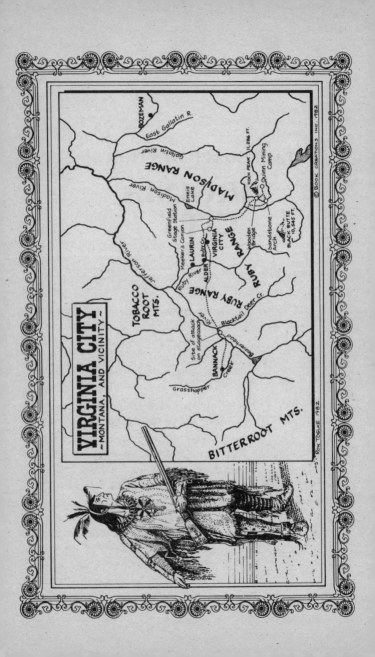

Chapter 1

The stage road from Bannack to Virginia City, Montana, was a lonely trace, hemmed in by sagebrush and surrounded by steep, barren hills. It ran through the desolate valley of the Beaverhead River, heading northeast to the Ruby Mountains, where mining camps boomed during the gold rushes fifteen years earlier.

Back in the 1860s, prospectors swarmed over the hills of southern Montana Territory, cutting this road in their stampede for gold. Along its route, they left memories of their passing—a pile of stones over a forgotten grave, a broken wheel rotting in a thicket. At a bend in the trace near the river's bank lay a rusted pan, the flat, broad kind used by miners to wash pay dirt from streams. It might have dropped from a mule pack on the way to Alder Gulch, or perhaps it was thrown aside as useless by a disgusted fortune hunter.

However the old pan came to be at the side of the stage road, it was off the rutted track and might have lain undisturbed for years if it had not been hit by a speeding stagecoach that took the bend too quickly and too wide. The right front wheel struck the pan, sending it rattling against a rear wheel with a clang that startled Gwen Quinn, who sat in the box next to the driver. Gwen was shaken out of her thoughts, and she gasped when the stage bounced over a rock, jarring her again, as her exhausted body had been jarred so often since they had left Bannack just before dawn, eleven hours ago. This last leg of her long journey was turning out to be the hardest of all.

Hawk Devlin was whining again, complaining that he was sorry he had ever agreed to drive the coach. "What a man's got ter do fer a livin'! Never woulda gone along with this if I'd of knowed this was such a hard-mouthed, mangy team! Never woulda tooken this damned job if I'd of knowed this rig was so used up. . . ." He was a beak-nosed, dirty man, older than his years, whose native Missouri learning was limited to the language of a keelboat roustabout.

He hurried the team up a long grade and cracked the whip over the struggling right-wheeler. "Pull, you sonofabitch! Earn yer feed, yuh mangy cayuse! I seed better horseflesh in a glue factory! Heeyah! Get along!"

Out of the corner of his eye, Hawk Devlin peered at Gwen, who ignored him and looked away at the shallow river on its way to the Jefferson and later the muddy Missouri. She heard Devlin snicker and felt his eyes search her.

Then she stared hard and cold at him, her hands clenched into fists on her knees. "Watch the road, driver."

Again, he snorted and snickered, using the whip and pressing the horses on. It was no wonder Devlin looked so closely at Gwen, for at twenty-one she was a beautiful woman. Her blond hair was pinned up under a beige Stetson, and her clothes—denim jeans and soft boots, a man's red flannel shirt and a sheepskin jacket—concealed the lithe lines of her body. But her face, with those bright blue eyes and high cheekbones, the full lips and delicate nose, attracted any man who knew beauty. Even gnarled old Devlin, who had long ago given up any hope of having a beautiful woman, found it hard to keep his eyes from her.

The coach rose up the steep grade to higher ground above the river, and the world changed from the shining gray of sagebrush hills to cool hues of blue and white. The distant peaks of the Madison Range came into view beyond the Rubys, away to the east, and Gwen's heart lifted. The sight of those mountains, all snow covered and gleaming in the crisp air of autumn, thrilled her, for she was almost home.

After six weeks and fifteen hundred miles—to Denver, back to Salt Lake City, and up to Bannack again—Gwen Quinn's mission was nearly complete. As she lurched and swayed in her seat next to the foul-smelling driver she had hired along with this coach in Bannack the previous night, Gwen recalled those weary days—days of keeping a hundred appointments, of telling about her father's gold mine, again and again repeating the same tale of hope and hard work until the sentences and phrases had poured from her without thought.

But she had succeeded! Her father's family, his friends, old business connections, and even a few strangers who believed Gwen Quinn's promises of striking it rich had given her money. They had invested ten thousand dollars in Quinn Mining Enterprises, and now all Gwen had to do was get back to the Madisons and her father's hard-rock mine. Then he could pay his disgruntled miners—men who had not seen a greenback from their employer in three months. The ten thousand dollars was down inside the stage, in a small strong-box guarded by her cousins, Caleb and Silas Quinn.

Gwen gazed at those distant blue mountains—still sixty miles away—with a feeling of joy. There, at the southern base of Koch Peak, lay her father's gold mine. With this money, Gwen could give her father another start in life, could give him hope. After all he had suffered, all the setbacks and the heartbreak, he deserved whatever his daughter could do for him.

The stage hit a washout and jarred her again, and she grasped the side bar of her seat to keep from bouncing off. She thought she should have become used to stage travel by now, but this leg of the trip was even more tiring than crossing the high pass of the Beaverheads to the south. Perhaps it was the reckless way Devlin drove, pounding over boulders and racing through curves without a care for the stage or the team.

The coach and horses were Gwen's responsibility, and she had left a healthy deposit of six hundred dollars at the stage-line office in Bannack when she leased them. Stagecoach was the fastest way to reach the mine with the load of supplies and the two hundred pounds of dynamite Gwen had bought in Bannack. But there was no one other than Hawk Devlin in that town who could handle a four-horse team—at least no one willing to risk the Indians.

Devlin reached into a side pocket of his old, battered coat and uncorked a bottle. Gwen wanted to tell him not to drink, but she held back because he might refuse altogether to finish the trip—might even head back to Bannack and leave them stranded there.

He took a greedy swig and did not spill a drop, even though the stage lurched and swayed as the team balked at his clumsy handling of the reins while he guzzled.

"Get along, fly bait!" Devlin roared, and belched. He fumbled the cork back onto the flask of Valley Tan and slipped the bottle into his pocket, leering at her again.

At last, Gwen could take it no longer. Shaking off her weariness, she took the Stetson from her head and held it down to the stage window, calling to Caleb. A hand took the hat from her, and she nimbly swung down from the box and stuck her legs through the window.

Then she was inside, sitting with a pair of burly fellows in their early twenties. By contrast with the grimy, surly Devlin, they were clear eyed and clean. Caleb, the younger, was a curly-haired giant, thickly muscled, with an open, friendly face. Silas was the older, more serious but equally as handsome as his brother. The floor of the coach was crowded with burlap sacks of supplies for the mine, and Gwen's cousins sat opposite each other with their legs extending across the bags to the other seat. The dynamite was in the canvas-covered boot.

"Thought you'd be comin' down from there sooner," said Caleb, who sat next to her. He offered a slice of Utah apple and said, "Been up there near two hour, Gwen. How can you stand bein' so close to that old buzzard?"

Gwen chewed on the apple. "Got to see he knows the way, Caleb. He's drinking now, and I'm afraid he'll take a wrong turn and we'll be in Idaho tonight."

"Okay," Caleb said, and wiped his hands on his shirt. He reached for his jacket and said, "Guess it's my turn to ride shotgun. Don't seem right, though, that I should be watchin' out for our driver as well as for Injuns."

As Caleb hung out the stage window, Silas looked up from a copy of Twain's *Roughing It* and said, "Give me an hour, little brother, then I'll take a turn."

When Caleb was gone, up on the box with Devlin, Gwen leaned her head back against the seat padding and closed her eyes. She let her hand slip down until her fingers felt absently under the seat for the eight-inch-square steel strongbox.

"It's still there, cousin," Silas said in his slow way.

She opened her eyes and gave him a rueful smile, then closed them again and let the rocking-chair rhythm of the coach swinging on the leather thoroughbraces lull her to sleep.

Time passed, although Gwen did not realize it. She lurched awake suddenly as the coach rocked from side to side and Devlin's nasal screeching came down. Caleb sat across from her now, his feet up on the pile of canvas sacks. She sat forward, her heart thudding from the abrupt awakening, and looked out the window.

"Just fording the Beaverhead," Caleb said to soothe her. "A bit more and we'll be turning up Blacktail Deer Creek, and tomorrow to the mountains."

"At last," Gwen said, and stretched out her stiff legs, which also lay on the supply bags. "We'll be back at the mine the day after tomorrow if Devlin can drive the mountain road the way he says he can."

Caleb pulled a harmonica from his shirt, saying, "He said he could last night when he'd had a deal of Valley Tan in his gut."

Gwen held on to the sway straps as the coach splashed through the ford. "Maybe he needs Valley Tan to know how to drive."

"But likely he never come this way before, drunk or sober. He used to drive for Ben Holladay, and Holladay never ran a feeder line to any mines. No profit in it."

Gwen's words were chopped up by the rude jerking of the coach. "Likely Devlin never . . . would have come this way at all if . . . we'd waited till sunrise to leave. If he'd sobered up before he started driving, I do believe . . . his fear of the Indians would have changed his Missouri mind for him."

"I tell you, Gwen, that driver's feared to death of Injun trouble; says there's been a smart lot of Injun trouble lately, especially on the road we're takin'." Caleb put the harmonica in his lap and rummaged through a picnic basket on the floor for one of the corn muffins they had packed. He tossed one to Gwen, who dug out a piece of cheese for herself. The stage was pulling up onto dry land again.

He spoke through a mouthful of food. "Devlin says three wagon parties goin' up to our mine was attacked and the teamsters just got out alive, most of 'em. I tell you, that driver's got the shivers up and down his spine every time a cloud drifts over, and after what I heard in Bannack about the Injuns, I can't say I blame him."

They ate in silence for a while as the stage ran along the smooth flood plain of the east bank of the Beaverhead. Gwen had heard talk about hostiles—Crows, it was thought—causing trouble in the foothills of the Madisons. It seemed that all the recent convoys heading up to her father's mine had been forced to turn back, and the independent stage operator who had a small line to the gold and silver mines in the region had refused to run a regular stage up there because of the danger. That was why Gwen had been forced to lease this rickety old veteran from him—and pay the deposit as insurance against loss of the vehicle.

She tried to sleep again but could not. When Devlin stopped to rest the horses and water them, she changed places with Silas and got back up in the box once more. She was grateful for the company and protection of Caleb and Silas Quinn. Only they knew about the ten thousand dollars in the strongbox, and she could count on them without a doubt.

Inside the coach were two loaded Winchesters, and a third lay at Gwen's feet. She knew well how to use it. Each of her cousins had a pistol at hand, but neither was a real gunfighter. They were miner's sons who had spent their lives in mining camps, first in Colorado and Nevada and now in Montana. Like their father before them—a man killed in the same cave-in that had badly injured Gwen's father last summer—

they had always failed to strike it rich. But now there was hope. That was what the dynamite was for: Tom Quinn was sure there was a fabulously rich vein of gold just beyond a wall of quartz, but there was no way to get to it without blasting. Since supplies and mining gear had not come through recently because of the Indian troubles, Gwen and her cousins had brought this dynamite with them, knowing that her father was already short of it when first they had departed for Denver.

If that vein could be opened, they would all be rich. Tom Quinn could pay off the syndicate of Salt Lake City businessmen that held the mortgage to the mine, and all the backbreaking work and the Quinn family's losses would be compensated for at last. Gwen did not care so much for fortune as she did for the welfare of the father she loved so. She had made him promise to give up mining after the Black Butte strike came through, and he had agreed to buy a hotel outside Denver and settle down there to a more peaceful life. But if the gold vein were not struck soon, then all her father had labored for would be lost, and she feared for his health, for his very life, if that happened.

For a moment, Gwen prayed that the miners had not walked out on her father yet. Since they had not been paid for so long, they would be angry and rebellious—even more so now than when she had gone away. If the miners were to leave her father, he could not break through to the new vein. Winter would set in before he could hire replacements with the money Gwen was now taking to him, and the heavy debts owed to the mining syndicate in Salt Lake would have to be paid off with the cash Gwen had raised in the past six weeks. If that money went for mortgage payments, then there would be nothing left for operating expenses, and the Quinn mine would be unworkable. After so much sacrifice, Tom Quinn would have to sell out, and the buyers would surely be the syndicate, which held the right of first refusal.

Gwen shook away these thoughts and looked out at the gray-green sagebrush shimmering in the setting sun. Shadows were lengthening and deepening in the gullies of the Ruby Range, and the eastern mountains were rosy at their peaks. Fields of new snow glowed warm on the high meadows, and the ragged summits sparkled where granite cropped through. The bases of the round-topped Rubys were already in the shadow of the Bitterroot Mountains to the west.

When they reached the Blacktail in a half hour or so, they planned to stop and make camp. Gwen wished they could travel on through the night, but this was no ordinary stage run, with convenient stations every ten or fifteen miles supplying a new team of fresh horses. They had to make do with what they had, and she hoped an animal would not go lame or the coach be damaged.

As Gwen took her turn alongside the driver, neither cousin thought to tell her a woman should rest. They knew Gwen Quinn too well for that. She could ride and shoot as well as any man, and she did her fair share of whatever work was at hand. She didn't do actual quartz mining, but the endless chores of business management and mining camp organization were in her hands, and she was good at them.

The river was swinging east now, and soon they would come to Blacktail Deer Creek's fork. Now, thought Gwen as she felt drowsiness come over her again, they were really pointing toward home. The Madison Range was in front of them, the sun setting behind them. Inside the coach, Caleb was playing a mellow tune on his harmonica. For the first time in six weeks, Gwen Quinn allowed herself to believe that her journey had an end, one that was coming soon. Without being aware of it, she began to doze.

A rifle cracked! Shock ran through Gwen's body, and she burst into wakefulness. Devlin shrieked horribly, but he was not hit, just terrified. Bullets zinged and whined past her head as she reached down into the front boot, fumbling for the Winchester. The men inside the stage were firing back. Devlin was babbling in terror, his body shuddering with convulsions. The horses broke stride and let back in the traces, and the stage began to slow. Another bullet sang past, and more struck the stage. Devlin began to rant at the horses, whipping madly.

Gwen came up with the rifle and turned against the seat back, looking into the glare of the sun. She could just make out the dust and shadows of riders galloping down a slope sixty yards away. She concentrated, heart pounding, trying to aim while the stagecoach bounced and barreled along the rutted trace. They were Indians, all right, at least six of them, rapidly closing, already riding through the dust of the stage.

She aimed at the lead warrior, her sight jumping up and down with the motion of the coach, and fired. A miss. It was impossible to shoot accurately while the stage was moving. She fired, levering the action, fired, and fired and fired again, wildly. Still the Indians came on, none hit, their own shots passing close to the fleeing coach. Her cousins were letting go as well, but without any better luck.

Suddenly, Devlin shrieked again. Gwen spun to see three more mounted Indians spread across the road ahead. On her right, two of the pursuing Indians were passing the coach at thirty yards' distance, riding for the same spot in the road where the other braves were gathered. The stage was cut off!

In a desperate move, Devlin turned the team to the left, off the trace and into sagebrush, driving up the ravine of a dry stream bed. The horses slowed, fighting their bits, frightened by the gunfire, trying not to stumble on this rougher ground.

"Got to fort up!" Devlin shrieked. "Got to fort up fast! Fast!"

As sagebrush and cottonwood branches skimmed past the bouncing coach, Gwen felt fear rise within her. This detour might end with the coach turned over at the mercy of the Indians, but it was too late to change directions now. She would have driven straight ahead if she had been the driver. She would have charged right through the Indians. . . . It worried her to see the ravine deepen, with steep slopes on both sides rising above the stage. If they had to fort up, as Devlin said, this was no place to do it. Indians could get up there and shoot down on them with ease. But now there was nothing for it but to run, to hope the ravine eventually opened into flat ground and there find a defensible position.

Devlin shrieked again and tramped on the brake, standing up in the box, hauling with all his might on the reins. Gwen saw why: Three more Indians were partly concealed by willows, all dismounted and waiting for the stage to run under their guns. As Devlin pulled up, the team fought him and stumbled. He tried to turn them to escape back the way they had come, but the stage slid sideways under the force of the maneuver. It heeled over and fell with a splintering crash on its side. Gwen barely managed to leap clear as the stage went down, its wheels spinning. She held on to her rifle and scrambled to her feet, shaken and half stunned, her hat gone.

The sound of screaming horses and flying lead brought her back. She was forty feet from the overturned stage, and she dashed for its cover. Bullets whined, and a few raised dust near her feet. The team was struggling and plunging in the traces, the terrified horses kicking and squealing. Gwen was relieved to see Silas jump from the coach's door and attack the leathers with a knife. Caleb came right behind him, rifle and canteen in hand, ducking behind the stage. The center coach pole that held the team fast had splintered at the front wheels, but the harness and reins had tangled on the axle, preventing the horses from getting away. Then, as Silas's knife flashed, the animals gave a panic-stricken leap and broke free, but they were still hitched together. They set off, racing farther up the narrowing end of the ravine. Gwen found herself huddled behind the coach bottom with Caleb and Silas at her side. A quick glance told her that Silas had been kicked hard by the struggling horses when he cut them free and that his head was bleeding. Caleb peered over the top of the coach, searching for the Indians.

Gwen gasped for breath and looked around. "Where's Devlin?"

"Back there," Silas said, sounding stiff and in pain; the wind was gone from him, for a horse had also kicked him in the ribs.

Gwen saw the driver's dark, twisted body lying unmoving against a prickly pear cactus. Without speaking, she turned away again. Now the firing had stopped. Not an Indian was in sight. Except for the pounding hooves of the stage team charging away up the ravine, there was no other sound. Then Silas coughed, and Gwen saw him grimace with pain.

A mile farther up the stage road, a tall man dressed in a buckskin shirt and wearing the floppy leather hat of a buffalo hunter stood near his horse, listening to the gunfire. The big black and white Appaloosa gelding pricked up its ears and whickered as it heard the flurry of shots from back down the trail. Nearby, in a glade of cottonwoods at the edge of Blacktail Deer Creek, the man's packhorse, not yet unloaded for the camp he intended for that peaceful spot, whinnied nervously.

Grant Jordan stepped away from the edge of the stream and

removed his hat, giving his attention to the sound of shots being carried on the wind. He was weathered, lean and strongly built. His sandy hair was short, his brown eyes alight with the keen intelligence of a man who has long counted on his wits for survival. The Appaloosa whickered again and pawed the ground.

"You ready to go, big friend?" he asked the animal, thinking that the Nez Percé bred their war-horses well—this one's fighting spirit was up already, as though he knew the sound of gunfire meant trouble. Perhaps, thought Jordan, the big fellow smelled blood.

In a few swift movements, Jordan hobbled a forefoot and hind foot of the packhorse and spoke gently, telling the mare to remain there until he came back. He snatched the Remington .50 hunting rifle from its scabbard at the side of the packhorse and loaded it. Then he was up on the Appaloosa and moving back down the trail—not too quickly, for another man walking into an ambush would do no one any good.

At Jordan's hip was a Colt Peacemaker, and in the scabbard on his saddle was a loaded Winchester. His saddlebags held a couple of days' food, and he had a full canteen just in case this encounter lasted some time. He also had Confederate cavalry binoculars slung in a pouch on his saddle.

The Appaloosa, white on its face and spotted on its rump but a shining black on legs, chest, and body, was young, excited, and unafraid. It began to canter, but its rider held it back, talking softly as he did so.

Grant Jordan rode like a man born to the saddle. As he trotted the Indian horse toward the sound of guns, he thought briefly of the Rebel cavalry company he had once captained. The gunfire sounded as though there were enough fighters mixing it up to warrant a few of the old unit at his back just then. But those days were long ago—more than twelve years now—when the world was younger and Virginians of his generation still had dreams. All those dreams had been wiped away at Yellow Tavern, gone and lost forever with the blood that flowed from J.E.B. Stuart, the finest leader a cavalryman could ever have. Since that day, Jordan had been on his own, an outcast, a man without roots, without dreams. Alone, he had handled whatever came his way, and he would do the same again right now.

Chapter 2

Caleb hung a belt of rifle rounds on the running gear and stood at the rear of the overturned coach. Gwen was near the front, lying on her side, aiming her rifle at the silent brush all around. Behind them, the ravine slope rose to an almost sheer, sandy cliff. It was Silas's responsibility at the center of the coach to watch that crest in case Indians came in behind them. If the attackers did that, there was nothing they could do to defend themselves, because they were exposed on that side. They knew it, and they figured the Indians knew it as well.

Still no shooting. In the distance, they heard the pounding of horses running down from the upper end of the ravine. It could be an attack, but probably it was the frightened team coming back. The three cousins watched and listened as the horses came nearer. Then the harnessed team came charging through the sagebrush, heedless of a clear path, crashing down everything in its way.

Someone out there shouted, and Gwen saw a figure leap up from cover and dart away from the stampeding horses. She brought up her rifle and in the same motion put two bullets into the man, and he went down hard. The team raced over him, flopping the body like a rag doll, leaving it worthless in the dust. Another Indian showed himself, and then another as the stage horses raced on by and plunged through the under-brush. Silas shot one man in the leg, and the other was lucky to get clear unhurt. The team thundered past the stage.

"That'll cramp their style!" Caleb chuckled. "Them varmints don't like to see their own people go under. Well, by golly, they'll lose more'n that afore this shindig's done."

Gwen watched the horses vanish in the sagebrush again, realizing sadly that the payroll would never get through to the mine now. . . . She stopped just short of thinking that none of them might get through at all.

A bullet sang past, and then the bushes came alive with gunfire. The three of them ducked as lead whizzed overhead, some bullets digging into the coach and punching right through its thin woodwork.

"This is a helluva fort!" Silas said as he stuck his finger into a hole near his head. "Come dark, we got to find better cover."

"See any?" Caleb asked.

Silas looked around the gulch. There was a clump of cottonwoods about sixty yards up the ravine, but likely the Indians would be there already. The ravine itself was less than one hundred yards wide, and back at its open end, where they had entered, the ground was level and overgrown.

"Maybe we can climb out over this bank behind us to-night," Silas said, looking up the slope behind the overturned coach. It was steep and sandy and would be hard to climb, but it might be done. Already, the sun was down behind the western mountains, and if the Indians didn't charge before total dark, they might just get up there and find a better place to defend themselves. The stage road was well traveled despite the dangers of hostiles, and sooner or later, someone was bound to come along and help out.

It was a slim chance, but it was their only one. The top of the slope behind them still had some light on it, and Silas watched closely for any sign of Indians up there. Sporadic shooting came from the brush in front of them, but as long as their enemy didn't get above them, they could hold out.

They heard the thunder of the galloping stage team coming back again.

"Now let's see how many of them varmints is slinkin' around in the bushes there," Caleb said, a grim smile on his face as he looked in the direction of the approaching horses, waiting for an Indian to move. Sure enough, one did just as the team bore down on him. Caleb missed, but Gwen shot him down in the brief instant that he showed himself.

The horses came on, crashing through the brush. Suddenly, a wall of fire met the animals as the Indians opened up on them, and all four went down screaming in a tangle of harness and flying legs. Gwen felt horror just then, seeing those poor animals shot like that. In the welling silence that seemed to rise up in the ravine after the horses were killed, she felt unable even to catch a breath. It was all like a dream, like a bottomless, falling nightmare! And there was Hawk Devlin! For all that he was, he was a man. . . .

And then it rose inside her like a clutching thing of ice. She realized she had already killed two human beings! She had actually killed two men! Despite her accustomed courage and self-confidence, Gwen Quinn began to tremble, thinking that this awful fear was more than she could handle . . . more than she ever wanted to know.

Another eruption of firing from the Indians, and Gwen and her cousins dived to the ground, faces pressed against the sand as bullets whacked and spattered all around them. Silas groaned, and Gwen felt cold fear again. She looked up and saw him holding his leg, bleeding from the thigh. She moved to where he leaned against the coach, and Caleb made a weak reply to the gunfire with his pistol.

As Gwen tore at the tough denim of the pants leg, she felt her hands shaking uncontrollably. "Be okay, Gwen, it'll be okay," Silas said through gritted teeth. She tugged and tore, finally snatching her sheath knife out and ripping away the fabric until she saw the wound. It was bad. The leg was broken at the thigh. Silas could never walk out of here without help . . . he would never get up that slope after dark. She looked into his eyes. They were calm, steady. He smiled a little. "Don't worry," he whispered. "Don't worry."

Grant Jordan stopped the gelding where he saw the tracks of a stagecoach cut away to the right and vanish into a gulch. The shots were coming from down there.

He looked at the tracks of stage horses and unshod Indian ponies. It was strange that he had just passed this very spot twenty minutes before and had seen no sign of trouble. Why did the Indians let him pass if they were out for a fight? They wouldn't have missed a chance to get his hair, horses, and gear, would they? Or were they waiting just for this stage?

The gunfire had slowed down. Jordan looked over the terrain. He would best be able to see the fight from high ground. He spurred his horse ahead, riding up a gradual slope on the right of the ravine, moving quickly along for a hundred yards, keeping just below the crest so no one down in the ravine would see him. Then he dismounted and led the horse for a while, all the time listening to the shooting, guessing the number and type of weapons being used, and getting the lay of the land in mind. When he was satisfied that the trouble was close at hand, he hitched the gelding to a branch and took the army binoculars from his saddle. He slipped forward on his belly to the edge of the drop, yanking off his hat and peering over.

Down in the gathering shadows of the ravine, his binoculars found the overturned stage a hundred yards away, lying so that the top of the stage faced him. It took a while to make out the defenders on the other side of the coach. In the brush at the foot of the slope below Jordan were a dozen Indian ponies hitched together near an Indian sitting with a rifle, guarding the animals. He looked like a Crow, somehow, but not exactly like a Crow. The shirt and leggings were Crow, but the face . . . maybe Flathead? Half-breed? And the hair wasn't waist long the way a Crow brave wore it.

The whole scene came into Jordan's mind in an instant, and he quickly had the picture clear in his head. Marking the gunfire, he estimated at least ten Indians in the brush—he saw two lying dead. There might be others concealed by the thick scrub that covered the ravine floor.

Suddenly, there was a whoop of triumph from an Indian, and Jordan looked up to see a defender at the stagecoach throw up his hands and fall backward.

Gwen screamed, "Caleb! Caleb!" and leaped for him as he went down.

She dragged him back to the scanty shelter of the stage as the Indians fired and whooped. "Oh, Caleb, no, no!" she moaned, and pulled his head into her lap. Blood flowed over her from where the bullet had caught him in the temple. Silas was at her side, and she heard him whimper his brother's name once and fight back a sob.

"Cover us!" Silas said, taking the youth's head in his lap, and Gwen wrenched herself away to watch for an attack as Silas tended to him.

The Indians were laughing and screeching. One of them swore in English and called for them to give up. In fury, she leveled the rifle and emptied it in fifteen brutal seconds. Someone out there screamed in pain.

The silence that followed was disturbed only by the wind rattling the aspens. Light was fast fading in the gulch, although the sky was still blue overhead. Gwen trembled, afraid to turn to Silas, afraid to hear him tell her what she already knew. . . .

"He's dead," Silas's faint voice came to her, and Gwen shook until she had to bite a knuckle to stop her teeth from chattering. Silas dragged himself toward her; he was breathing short and fast.

"Better load that piece," her cousin said as he pulled himself painfully to stand behind the front wheel of the coach.

She searched for bullets in the cartridge belt Caleb had hung on the running gear, but there were none. She was angry with herself for wasting shells. Hands shaking, she looked at Silas, who said, "Take Caleb's six-shooter."

She put the Winchester down and picked up Caleb's pistol. She peered out at the brush; suddenly, she thought something moved at the crest of the slope on the other side of the gulch. But whatever it was had gone before she could take a bead on it. Anyway, the range was too far for a pistol to count for anything.

"I'll watch behind us," Silas said, and leaned with his back against the stage, rifle in hand.

For a few more minutes, while the Indians picked their shots now and again, Gwen stood in silence, not willing to waste another shell. She thought about stories old-timers told—stories about fighting Indians and what you could expect if you were taken prisoner. *Keep one bullet for yourself*, they always said. That warning never seemed anything to think twice about before, even though she had lived near Indian trouble in Montana Territory for five years—a period divided in half by two years spent back East in Philadelphia at that foolish finishing school.

Finishing school! She smiled to herself now, wryly and cynically, thinking of the girls she had known in Philadelphia. They were society girls and each of their life's ambition was to be a lady: the lady of a governor, of a legislator, or of a Washington dignitary. Ladies, all! What would they say now? What would they say about Gwen Quinn when they heard she had been killed by Indians out in the wild West?

Probably not much more than they had said about her, and to her, already. Her mind drifting, she recalled that warm spring day when she'd had enough—the day she packed and stormed out of the ivy-walled school for governors' ladies and took the first train back to St. Joe. Not much more the ladies could say about her being mad, but her death would make for good tearoom conversation, it would. She ducked instinctively as a fusillade of shots struck the coach.

Bitterness rose up and quickly sank in her. Gwen felt so very tired. The pistol in her hand was almost too much to hold. She felt as though she had not the strength to pull the trigger. . . . Wait! There, on the rise across the ravine! Something moved that time for sure! She looked closer, and it was hard to tell, but she thought she saw a white man mount up and disappear on the other side of the crest!

Her heart lifted. Someone was there! Someone to help or to go for help.

"Silas!" she called softly. "There's someone there. Someone to help, I think!"

But there was no reply. "Silas?" She looked around. Silas Quinn was slumped against the rear axle, blood soaking his chest, shot by a bullet that had ripped through the coach.

Terrified, Gwen fell to his side. His eyes opened slightly. "Gwen," he rasped. "I'm done. . . . But you got to get away! Listen . . .'' She hushed him with a drink of canteen water. He tried to speak again.

"No," she said quickly. "No, don't talk, Silas. Don't give up! There's someone . . . a white man out there. . . ."

But Silas seemed not to hear. The water ran out of his mouth and brought blood with it. He looked at her, and his eyes begged. "Gwen . . . don't let them take you . . . hear! Promise me . . . promise me that . . . Shoot your . . ." He groaned in pain. "Oh, girl, what . . . what have we done?"

Then his head lolled, and he was gone. Gwen went blank. She did not know how long she knelt at her cousin's side, but a bullet banged against the stage and startled her back to her senses. She was alone now. They would come soon. Silas was right. They must not take her alive.

A thought came suddenly! If she burned the stage, then the explosion of the dynamite in the boot might cause enough confusion for her to make it up the near ridge! She cast a glance quickly at the steep wall of sandy soil. Yes, that just might work! But all the money . . . all her labors . . . First she had to climb into the stage under fire and get the small strongbox. She would not leave it behind, not now, not after it had cost so much. . . .

Once more she looked across the gulch at the opposite height of ground, wondering if the white man she thought she had seen was really there. But nothing moved, and in the gathering dimness it would have been difficult to see anything that did not move. She had to act. There was no time to wait for help that might not be there. She must get the strongbox out of the coach!

Gwen took a deep breath. Her mouth was dry, and she felt weak in her legs. But . . . In one instant, she was thinking about this desperate attempt, and in another she was scrambling headfirst into the coach door. Bullets cut savagely, wickedly through the stage, where Gwen huddled on the bottom, sitting on the ground through the open window, the strongbox held close to her. A bullet pinged and whined close to her head. She realized her eyes were tightly closed, and when she opened them, the dimness gave her the terrifying thought that the hostiles might at that very moment be taking the chance to slip up on her. She had to get out as she had come in, but first she fumbled for matches and Silas's book. . . .

Grant Jordan had led his horse down the side of the gulch at the narrow end of the ravine. Keeping to a watercourse that cut deeply into the slope, he was sheltered now from the fighting, and neither the defenders at the stage nor the Indians could see him as he slipped through a crowd of cottonwoods and thick sagebrush. Then he stopped the horse and swept the binoculars over the floor of the gulch. Two bodies lay near the coach a hundred yards away. He saw someone's legs disappear into the stage. That was a bad place for the only survivor to hide. The Indians could pour lead into it.

But it seemed that only a few redskins had seen their quarry's movement, and no more than three guns took shots at the stage in the hope of a chance hit. Here at the head of the gulch, the walls of the ravine sloped up on both sides of Jordan. In some brush on the left, sixty yards away, the Indian ponies were bunched, and he could see the swishing of a tail there. He drew the Winchester from its scabbard and put away the big buffalo gun.

Just then, he saw movement on top of the slope behind the stage. An Indian! From where he stood, Jordan made out the man against the dull sky. When the fellow in the stage tried to get out, he would be an easy target. Jordan had to act now.

He swung up the rifle, took aim, and fired. His second shot was one too many. The redskin on the ridge flew backward, legs and arms flying. The next four quick shots were sent at the Indian horses, the bullets ricocheting and cracking against rocks, startling the already nervous animals. As he mounted, Jordan saw several horses pull away, whinnying, and one, apparently hit, was screaming like a wind devil. Then they broke out, stampeding into the gully.

At that moment, the fellow inside the stage threw himself out the door and landed hard on the earth. Jordan gave a rebel yell that rose loud and piercing above the din of the horses and spurred the Appaloosa on, charging for the stagecoach.

Gwen gasped for breath after she thudded to the ground. The strongbox had bruised her ribs when she made her leap from the coach door. Then she heard a bloodcurdling yell— the familiar battle cry of Confederate soldiers that had often sounded near the farm before the Quinns fled the bloody Shenandoah Valley. No redskin screeched like that.

The Indian ponies ran frightened and circling through the sagebrush. The rebel yell exploded again, this time only fifty yards away. Out of the undergrowth came a giant horse, thundering right at her.

"Get aboard!" its rider blared.

Guns were going off. Men were shouting, horses neighing and rearing. The Appaloosa descended on Gwen like a huge black phantom. Without thinking, she jammed the small strongbox into her shirt and got ready for the leap. The rider was hanging at the right side of the horse, Indian style, one arm hooking out to help yank her up. There was no time to stop and mount—there was only one way to get on.

Now! The horse pounded near the stage. Gwen ran alongside for a moment, caught the arm, and threw her legs up, struggling to get her left foot over the saddle, trying to pull herself up behind the rider.

Jordan pushed her over the horse's back, shouting, "Keep low! Keep low!"

Gwen got her left leg over the saddle, held her heel against the cantle, and leaned forward, shoulder just touching the back of the horseman, who was still slung at the side of the animal's neck. Bullets whined and zipped close enough to make her wince. Cottonwood branches and sage stung her as they rode, but the horse seemed to know the way to safety even though the evening was deep now, with a purple haze on the horizon over the long crests of the black Bitterroot Mountains.

This was a hell of a good horseman, thought Grant Jordan. At his back, he felt the light, skillful rider, who had leaped on perfectly, without the Appaloosa missing a stride. The wind whipped against Jordan's face as he called back, "Straighten up now! We're on our way outa here!"

They sat up in the saddle, Gwen behind him, and the horse ran even faster. It would take time for the Indians to catch their own horses and come after them. Jordan intended to break for Blacktail Deer Creek, pick up the packhorse, and flee northeast into the rugged Ruby Range, headed for Virginia City.

They rode for another five minutes, neither speaking. Then Jordan reined in the gelding and slowed to listen for any pursuit. Only the sound of the Beaverhead rushing past could be heard over the blowing of his mount. No other hoofbeats.

He spurred the horse again but jerked to a stop when a great explosion broke in a series of sharp claps behind them and the night lit up with yellow and red fire from the gully, now half a mile away.

"What the hell was that?" Jordan asked as his horse whinnied with fright.

"Dynamite," Gwen replied, so softly that he could hardly hear her voice.

"What you say?"

"Dynamite. The stage was loaded with—"

"Hey! You're a woman! Why—"

Gwen said nothing. She felt limp and useless now. Her body ached. Her weary legs and arms were spent. A rush of faintness dizzied her, and it was all she could do to hold on to Jordan's waist.

He said, "I say you're . . . I mean . . . are you all right, ma'am?"

By her voice and the way she rode, he knew she was young. And by the way she had fought, she was very brave . . . and very good with a gun. Jordan was impressed. In the darkness, he could not see her face when he turned slightly to repeat his question. He wondered what a woman like this looked like.

But she did not reply. He felt her head against his back, her hands clutching tightly to his shirt. She seemed heavy for the first time.

"Ma'am? Ma'am, you all right? You hit?"

Gwen jerked back to consciousness.

"What? Oh, no . . . no. I'm all . . . I'm . . ." The sobs came, unexpected and powerfully, compelling her to release the utter desolation she felt. "Oh . . . I . . . I . . ." She could not catch her breath. "I'm . . . I . . ." A sob held her words back as she struggled to speak.

"It's all right, ma'am," Jordan said, and he spurred the horse toward the creek where the packhorse was hobbled. "Just hang on. We'll get out soon . . . and everythin'll be just . . ." Jordan hesitated, because he knew that nothing would ever be the same for this woman after what she had come through. He knew his words would sound empty, but he said them, anyway: "It's all right. Just hang on, ma'am. We'll be all right soon. Hang on."

They rode into the night, hardly speaking, both very tired. Only the Appaloosa seemed untroubled by the day's labors.

Once he was sure the girl was unhurt, Jordan bent all his efforts to getting them away from there. He was familiar with this country, having passed through several times while traveling between the northeastern plains and Utah Territory to the south or between the Yellowstone country in the southeast and the mountains of the Nez Percé in the west.

In the darkness, the horse picked its way cautiously over the flats at the foot of the knobby Ruby Mountains, moving steadily northeast. They would stop and rest when Jordan figured they were close to a trail he knew that cut across the Rubys and led down to Virginia City, a mining town tucked away in the middle of the mountains. He felt saddle weary and drained. It would be good to stop soon.

Gwen was alert now, though her body was numb with fatigue. Her mind raced, anxiety twisting her thoughts as she speculated on what this man was all about. Hidden between them in her shirt was the small strongbox with ten thousand dollars in it. What would he do if he saw the box? What would she tell him about it? Did she owe money to him in exchange for saving her life?

He was quiet, this man. He spoke seldom, and then only to ask if she wanted to rest. She did not. She wanted to put distance between herself and the horror of the ravine, where poor Caleb and Silas lay dead.

Tears ran down Gwen's cheeks, and she sighed shakily. She sniffed and rubbed her face with a shirt-sleeve. Jordan half turned to her, seemed to think better of it, then stopped the Appaloosa.

He dismounted, bringing his leg forward over the horn to avoid bothering Gwen with his roweled spurs. In the starlight of the clear, high mountain night, she saw him leading the horse. He was a big man, the kind who belonged on a horse like this one. She saw the glint of light on the rifle in his hand.

"Can I hold that weapon for you, sir?" she asked after clearing her throat. "It's the least I can do if you let me ride. . . ."

"It's all right, ma'am. We'll be stopping soon. I hear a stream ahead, and we can refresh ourselves a bit before moving on."

As she rocked gently in the saddle, Gwen thought about that voice. Southern, that was sure. Well bred, she guessed; likely once a gentleman. But would this stranger be a gentleman when he saw the strongbox? It was hard and uncomfortable against her ribs. It would be difficult to conceal from him for long. She wished they would get to Virginia City soon.

"Sir," she called, and saw his shadowed form turn to her as he led the horse.

"Ma'am?"

"Would it be possible to go on all through the night? Could we try to reach Virginia City . . . perhaps before dawn?"

Jordan thought about that for a moment. Then he answered, "No, ma'am. We're another seven hours from there, that's certain. I won't play out my horses, and I won't risk going over a cliff up in the mountains. I understand your wish to get there, ma'am, but you'll have to be patient. We'll reach the town before noon, I'd say. But we'll need to rest the animals for a few hours. Likely you could use some rest yourself."

They came to a brook that shimmered in the darkness, reflecting the stars. She swung down from the horse, and her aching legs gave way as she reached the ground. Jordan caught her up, lifting her a little, his arm pressing the strongbox hard against her side. She spun away to keep the box out of his reach and forced herself to stand, taking short breaths and shaking her head slowly as she fought for self-control and balance.

"Thank you . . . I'm all right. . . ."

He stood back. "Best sit at the stream. I'll water the horses. You sleep. We'll ride on in a couple of hours." He moved off into the darkness.

Gwen felt her legs yielding again, but she struggled to regain some strength. She edged away from where the man and the horses were busy at the water. Her foot knocked against a stone, and she nearly fell. She heard him tell her to be careful.

Gwen dropped to her knees on a clump of thick bunchgrass. This would serve her purpose. She would conceal the box in the grass until they were ready to go, then retrieve it, slip it into her shirt once more, and keep it hidden there until they got to Virginia City. She unbuttoned her flannel shirt, slipped the box out, and tucked it into the grass. A chill suddenly rushed through her as she thought that a rattler might be there. Carefully, slowly, she concealed the box.

With a deep, deep sigh, she sat down. For the first time, she felt the cold chill of the Montana mountains, and she shivered. But with the strongbox hidden, she could at least sleep without worrying that this man would find it.

"This will keep you warm," the man said, and she looked up, surprised to see his dark outline against the sky. How long had he been there? Before Gwen could take the blanket he was offering, she felt fright again, thinking that perhaps, in his frontiersman way, this fellow had seen through the dark and had observed her hiding the box.

He laid his saddle down, and she lay back on it for a pillow. At her left shoulder was the bunchgrass and the payroll her father so desperately needed. Over her was the stranger's woolen blanket, warm and protective. She wondered then what his name was. She would ask later. Later. . . . Before she had time to think of the day's sorrow, Gwen Quinn fell into a sound and dreamless sleep.

*   *   *

As he sat with his back against a fallen cottonwood trunk, Grant Jordan peered through the darkness at the girl, who was now sleeping. He drew his extra saddle blanket close and brought his knees up, wishing they could safely light a fire for warmth.

In the distance, a coyote howled, moaning and yowling in a lost and lonely way. Another answered from up in the Ruby Mountains, telling of men and horses in their hunting grounds. By dawn, there would be a pack of them slipping through the sagebrush nearby, making the mare restless and keeping Jordan awake. Just as well. He did not want to sleep too soundly tonight—the Indians might be on their trail even before daylight.

Jordan yawned. The mare whickered and stamped the ground as the first coyote yowled closer to the camp. The girl was too deep in sleep to hear it. Apparently, she felt secure, he thought. Likely she considered that bunchgrass to be a safe place for whatever it was she had so secretly hidden there.

Chapter 3

They were on the move again well before first light. Jordan had given Gwen some dried beef and hardtack with a swig of stream water to wash it down and canned peaches to give breakfast some life. It was a cold, windy predawn. Jordan had made a point of not asking what it was she had scrambled around in the grass for before she mounted behind him. It was her business, whatever it was, and Grant Jordan was a man who minded his own affairs and liked it that way. They still had not had a good, clear look at each other's faces—it had been dark or nearly so ever since the rescue the night before.

The trail led up and up, lurching and twisting through the forested mountains. Fir trees overhung the path, and even when the sun turned the eastern sky a mingled wash of blue and pink, the riders remained in darkness. Gwen was lost in thought, and she had almost forgotten that they still had not introduced themselves when Jordan said, "We haven't had the chance to do this right. . . . My name's Jordan, Grant Jordan."

31

"Pleased to meet you, Mr. Jordan," Gwen said, hearing her voice sound strangely formal, as though they were meeting at a tea social. Just then, they rode out from under the pine boughs and into an open stretch of trail, where the sun, though still below the horizon, had sifted gray light into the world. Jordan turned to face her, and under the floppy hat, his clear eyes were searching. Gwen met his gaze, and she saw a man who needed a shave but whose fine features and open face told of honesty and calm courage. "My name is Gwen Quinn."

He touched the brim of his hat, nodded, and turned back to the trail. She was, he thought, a very beautiful woman. He was looking straight ahead, but his mind held the image he had just seen over his shoulder: the fair hair, half pinned up, half straggling over her neck; the lovely face, tired and filled with sorrow but at once brave and spirited. And those eyes— he hadn't noticed the color, but the look of them, the depth and intensity there. That vision was enough to keep Jordan silent for another mile or so, and he thought about just what it was he had seen in those large eyes.

The sun peeked over the hills, and the mountain pass turned warm yellow and russet with the colors of September or aspens, willows, and sagebrush. It was then Jordan realized what he had seen in Gwen Quinn's eyes: hope—the kind of hope that comes from having a dream. That was the kind of hope Grant Jordan once had known in his lost generation of Virginians—a generation that had passed from an age of hope to an age of cynical, stubborn determination to survive, to go on living, to make a new life amid the ruins of a civilization that had gone up in flames.

Hope. Jordan knew that look, and he felt uneasiness to see it again in Gwen Quinn's pretty face. It reminded him too much of his own lost youth, of the time when his dreams were crushed forever. Since that terrible defeat, he had never been able to dream again or to conjure up an ideal to live by. Day to day. That was enough for Grant Jordan. Live from day to day and make the best of life. A good horse. Good country. Good hunting. Now and again, a good woman who would not ask too much of him. There was no place in that life for dreams or for hope. Soon, memories left Grant Jordan's thoughts, and he spoke to the Appaloosa as they moved into the warm sunlight pouring over the round-topped mountains. But the vision of Gwen's bright eyes stayed, lingering, before him.

They rode on slowly, steadily climbing over rocky, thickly wooded mountains, edging their way across steep slopes and under cliffs. They spoke more often now and told something of themselves—she about the mine and about the need for the dynamite destroyed on the stage, but she said nothing about the payroll. He said he was a professional hunter, heading north. Late in the morning, they came to a little widening of the trail where a stream picked its lively way down a rock face and ran across the path. Jordan stopped the horses and said, "There's no one coming after us. I've been looking back down the trail—" He motioned with a nod down the side of the mountain, and Gwen saw the track they had come up winding far below. "There's no one within miles. We've got an hour before we reach town. This is a good place to rest, freshen up, and eat something."

With that, Gwen dismounted, and he followed. As he led the horses to water, Gwen touched the bulk of the strongbox at her side. She was hatless to the sun and wind, and she suddenly realized that her hair must be in awful disarray. She felt for it and struggled to pin it up as she walked toward a little patch of grass.

The strongbox slipped from her shirt and dropped on her toe. The pain made her jump, but she bit her lip and restrained a cry of pain, quickly snatching up the box again and hurrying to the grassy spot. She tucked the box back into her shirt and felt Jordan's eyes on her, but she did not turn around.

Kneeling at the stream, she splashed cold water over her face and neck. It was refreshing but did nothing to relieve the deep unhappiness that had burrowed within her as if to stay there forever. It did ease her physical discomfort somewhat. Gwen had not rested well in a week of hard traveling from Salt Lake City. Ever since she began the final journey home, she had been haunted with fears, with doubt, and with a gnawing premonition of trouble. Well, now that trouble had come, and it had come more savagely than she had ever thought possible. *Silas. Dear Caleb. You didn't deserve this! You didn't.* . . . She buried her face in her hands and began to cry, out of control and miserable. She kept crying until Jordan came behind and said softly, "We ought to have a bite to eat, ma'am, then be movin' on."

She turned and looked up at him, not caring at all now about her tears, not trying to fight them back. Her shoulders shook, and her face went to her hands again. Jordan got down on one knee and put his arm around her shoulders, applying strong, gentle pressure, not saying a word. Then her forehead was against his buckskin shirt, her arms clutched her sides, and she let her tears flow unrestrained.

After a few moments, Jordan eased her back.

"I'm sorry . . . Mr. . . .Mr. . . . ah . . ."

"Jordan."

"Oh, I am sorry to behave like this. . . . You've done so much . . . I owe you— Why, Mr. Jordan, I've been such a fool that I've even forgotten to thank you for all you did yesterday! Please forgive me! If there's anything ever I can do . . ." She thought about the ten thousand dollars in the strongbox. Yes, he did deserve a reward from it, but not out here! She couldn't show it to him out here. . . . Or could she? Perhaps he could be trusted not to take advantage. . . . She looked up into his cool, forthright eyes. Perhaps she could tell him the truth. Her hand touched the box. She would need help to get to her father's mine. She would begin again, resupply, and buy more dynamite, and somehow she would get through. Perhaps this Grant Jordan would accept the job of escorting her.

Jordan saw that Gwen's mind was working clearly once more, that she had escaped the sadness that had come upon her so heavily. He smiled. This was a strong woman, indeed, to be able to keep herself from breaking down completely after the deaths of her cousins. Jordan's smile kept Gwen from offering the job. That smile was so distracting, so engaging, that it took her by surprise, and she found herself smiling back at him, although her mind was still whirling with confusion and sadness.

"Let's have some canned peaches, and you can repay me then—"

"What do you mean?" She stood up and backed off.

"I mean you can tell me how it is a pretty girl like yourself learned to shoot and ride like you do." He was smiling again, that same open-faced, guileless smile that had charmed her a moment before. He meant just what he said and nothing else. "I don't mean to pry into another's affairs, but I reckon you've got me puzzled." He went to fetch food from the packhorse.

"I mean," he continued as he opened a canvas bag of supplies, "You ride like an Injun, and you shoot like a man . . . better'n most men, and—" He stopped and looked closely at her, in a way that made her drop her eyes. "And you're mighty good-looking for such a good shot."

He brought out a can opener and took two cans of peaches to a flat rock, where he sat down and began to cut them open.

"Now, as I say," he continued slowly, "I don't like to put my oar in where it don't belong, but you do owe me something, Miss . . . ah . . ."

"Quinn," she said quickly, noticing immediately that he almost smiled when she did; perhaps his forgetfulness was intentional, she thought, evening the score because she had forgotten his name.

"Miss Quinn. Of course. Well, then, where do daughters of Montana miners learn to shoot and ride like you do?"

He handed her an open can and began to work on one for himself. She accepted it and sat at the stream, taking off her boots and dabbling her feet in the cool water.

"Yes, I do owe you something," she said, and drank some peach juice. "So I'll tell you." She fished out a slippery peach and savored the taste, refreshing and sweet. "I had an older brother, the apple of Pa's eye. He could ride like an Indian himself, and he taught me how as soon as I could walk. He didn't teach me how to shoot; I learned that out here. The family needed an extra gun now and again, and I sort of took to it in a natural way, though I'm not much with the pistol, really. I like the Winchester best." She drained off the last of the juice.

Jordan was finishing his own can of peaches as she spoke. "That brother must be a mighty fine teacher."

"He was."

"He with your pa at the mine? . . . No, I guess he's not, is he?"

Her head turned, and her eyes flashed. "You know so much, then?"

"Well, Miss Quinn, if your brother was out here, he would have been on that stage, not you, no matter how well you shoot."

She splashed her feet absently in the water, then said, "He was killed in the war."

Jordan tossed the can away. "A lot of good folk were. I reckon a lot of loyal Confederate folk from Shenandoah Valley had it tough in those days what with Sheridan and his rascals ridin' down on 'em time after time."

"He was *with* Sheridan," Gwen said too abruptly, without thinking. She looked up at Jordan again, but his face showed no emotion to hear that a son of Virginia had been a federal cavalryman.

He saw that tense sadness in her face once again, and he knew he had brought this conversation too far for both of them. He rose and stretched the stiffness from his legs. "Now we're even," he said softly. "Best be headin' down to town—Virginia City! Hah! That's quite an ambitious name for that place. I was last here two years ago, and that was long after the boom had gone bust. *City!* That's a high-reachin' description." He was tightening the cinch on the Appaloosa as he spoke. "And Virginia! It's sure no one from Virginia gave it that name! Must've been a slimy Yankee sympathizer comin' through who wanted to insult the Old Dominion—" He cut himself short, looked over his shoulder at Gwen, who was pulling on her boots, and said, "Sorry."

"For what?" she asked absently.

"Well, I guess all you Yankee sympathizers aren't slimy—"

"*Yankee?*" Gwen was on her feet, one boot in her hand. "You think I—that my family was for the Yankees?"

He cleared his throat. "Well . . . that looked to be the size of it—"

"*Yankee!*" She shook her head and gave an ironic laugh, then sat down on the rock again. She pulled on the other boot, then looked up at Jordan and said in a cool voice, "Only my brother was with Sheridan's raiders. My pa and ma and I were with Virginia, blood and fire! We pulled out of the valley because we lost everything! Everything! House, farm, friends, all gone. My brother was killed, too. And the

Shenandoah was lost to the Confederacy long before we left it. We came out here to start again, and that's what we've done, and we're trying to forget the war, to forget the hate and the dying and all we lost." She fought against a sob. "Just like I'm trying to forget what happened yesterday! We're trying to forget what happened twelve years ago!" She was shaking with anger, with pent-up emotion. "And that's why we're here, sir! We're not Yankee sympathizers, and we're not Rebel sympathizers anymore, either. We're from Montana Territory now, and this is where we'll stay, come hell or Indians or . . . or . . . Just don't go on to me about . . . about what's past!"

She broke down, sobbing again, and Jordan came to her side, but he did not touch her as he had before. He felt as though he had no right to hear what she had said. He tried to speak, but the words were not easy coming. "I'm sorry, Miss . . . ah . . ."

"Quinn!" she snapped at him, not lifting her head.

He stood over her for a moment, then, with pursed lips, knelt at her side. "See here, you're not the only one tryin' to forget," he said, and she looked at him with wet, running eyes. "I am sorry to start you up like this."

She shook her head. "No, Mr. . . . Jordan, I'm sorry. I'm very sorry. It's all been more than I'm able to bear."

She got up and went to the horse, standing there looking out at the mountains, waiting for Jordan to get on.

"You want this, don't you?" he asked from behind her.

She turned and gasped. He was holding out the strongbox. She took it quickly, pressing it close to herself. Her eyes searched his for a hint of something, anything, that would warn her to be on guard. But Jordan simply took the packhorse line in hand and mounted the Appaloosa. He gave her a hand and pulled her up. Whistling to himself, he headed the animal toward Virginia City.

* * *

It was a half hour later, not far from their destination, when Gwen spoke. She had thought it all over in her mind. Grant Jordan was unlike anyone she had ever met before, and although she knew nothing about him or his past, she sensed she could trust him.

"Would you like a job, Mr. Jordan?"

He cocked his head to listen. "A job?"

"Yes, working for me . . . I mean for Quinn Mining Enterprises."

"I got a job. Working for Grant Jordan, Limited. Buffalo hunter, guide to expeditions of European princes, maharajas of distant Jaipur, counts and contessas of Italy and Spain!"

"What are you on about?" She laughed, surprising herself that she could laugh at all just then.

"It's true, every bit of it," he said, and looked back at her with a bright gleam in his eye. He turned back to the trail and said, "Future kings, would-be sultans, geologists, plantologists, and anthropologists! True! Every bit of it!"

"Go on, Johnny Reb," she said.

"Go on, yourself, girl!" he protested, turning with a half grin and breaking into a backcountry drawl. "Why you ain't heard nothin' till you've heard the truth, an' that's what I'm peddlin', a right smart o' truth, though some mountain miners is too deef from blastin' to hear such things."

His voice was high as he teased her, breaking at the end, and Gwen laughed. "If this is all to cheer me up, Mr. Jordan . . . it's kind of you."

He faced the trail again and told her what he swore was the truth. Every spring, he went to Denver to take on an expedition of foreigners—tents and coaches, cameras and telescopes, camels and champagne, and generally enough wine to last a year if the guides weren't along and enough cattle on hand to keep a Sioux village in meat for months. His clients did not hunt game for the food but for the sport, for the hides and the racks. Each season, Jordan spent three or four months with expeditions on the plains or in the mountains, shooting game, visiting friendly Indians, touring the new national park at Yellowstone, earning a great deal of money while his noble patrons thoroughly enjoyed themselves in the wild American West. Fascinated, Gwen listened to his story, and for a while it was enough to make her forget her worries, if only for the short time it took to ride down out of the Ruby Range and stop on a bluff overlooking Virginia City.

"There it is," Jordan said. "Can't say I missed it since I was here last. Not even the name."

"Why did you come back, then?" Gwen asked, looking down at the drab sprawl of frame shanties, storehouses, blacksmith shops, hotels, and dance halls cluttering the floor of Alder Gulch far below them.

"I've a friend in the army, and he wrote me that his company will be stationed here for a few months until the trouble with the Nez Percé is over."

Gwen thought of the recent news that had caused a sensation all over the West: Chief Joseph of the normally peaceful Nez Percé, who lived across the Bitterroot Mountains, had defied the army and the government and was trying to avoid being herded onto a reservation. At that very moment, fewer than a hundred miles to the west of them, eight hundred men, women, and children of the Nez Percé were struggling eastward, fleeing soldiers who were pursuing them. They had defeated the army twice already in sharp fights.

"This horse is Nez Percé, isn't it?" Gwen asked.

"The very same," he replied. "Given to me by Joseph himself when I lived among them three years ago."

"What's he called?"

"Don't really have a name for him. The Nez Percé told me once, but I lost the handle. I tried namin' him a few times, but it never quite stuck. Few weeks ago, I tried callin' him Camas Meadows because of the battle Joseph won there, but the fightin's moved on since then, and there'll be other battles and other names. I just call him Injun horse . . . Injun works as well as any.''

They spent a few moments looking quietly down into Alder Gulch. The hills they stood on were lower than the steep slopes to the east and north. Off to the left was Ruby Creek, dammed where placer sluices ran water down to sift out what scarce gold remained from the great boom days of the mid-1860s. There wasn't much gold there now except in the miners' old slag heaps, where Chinese laborers toiled day after day, washing out what the white miners had long ago ignored, even scorned, and making a bare living out of it—but making a fortune for the rich hongs who hired the gangs of coolie laborers.

The big horse obeyed Jordan's touch and moved down a gravel slope toward the town. It was a steep slope, and slippery, with loose rock and dirt. Jordan was careful controlling the animal, which was having difficulty keeping its footing. He steered it to go less directly downward, but it slid, shaking its riders, and Gwen lurched dangerously in the saddle. She cried out as the strongbox bounced away down the slope, springing open with a clank and releasing wrapped bundles of hundred-dollar bills.

In a twinkling, she and Jordan were dismounted and skidding recklessly down the hill, little avalanches erupting from their feet, snatching up the money before it all blew away. It was a mad dash, and the wind played with the bills before they were caught. Then Gwen and Jordan sat down together, clutching handfuls of money, both breathless and scratched up from their exertions. Gwen's hair had lost its pins and hung full and glossy over her shoulders.

She stuffed her money into the box, and Jordan said with a

thoughtful look, "I see why you wanted to hide this box from me last night."

He handed her the rest of the cash, and she said nothing as she put it away and closed the lid.

"Was this what you jumped into the coach for when the lead was flyin'?"

She nodded.

"I guess I don't blame you. I'd do the same. But look, this ain't exactly tame country here, lady, and what you're carryin' will attract a lot of attention if you go on droppin' it down the sides of hills . . . even if you keep it stuffed in your shirt like you were doin'—that lumpy box doesn't look right to a man, not on you, believe me!"

Gwen looked embarrassed and said, "I do what I have to do. This money means everything to my father. Without it, all he has is lost . . . everything Caleb and Silas died for. I'm doing this the only way I can, the only way I know how, Mr. Jordan." She gave a weary, trembling sigh and brushed her hair back.

After a moment of sitting quietly while the horses grazed on some bunchgrass farther up the slope, Jordan said, "You'll have to find someone to help you. You can't go carrying that around alone, and you can't try to get through to the mine without more help than you had yesterday, that's sure."

"Mr. Jordan, will you help me?" She so hoped he would.

"That's the job I was about to offer earlier—"

"Hold on, Miss Quinn. Hold on! I'm a guide and a hunter, not an armed escort. Your mine lies south, but I'm headin' north before winter sets in. I've got travelin' to do before the snow flies, and I can't take the time to go south with—"

"I'll pay you well. Whatever you ask!"

"I don't need money," he said. "I told you, I get paid well for what I do. It's the kind of life I want, and I've a good lot of friends up in the Black Hills right now, men who're hunting game for the big minin' camps.''

He shook his head slowly, ''No, thanks. I'm movin' on after I meet my soldier friend down yonder.'' He indicated a little crowd of ten or fifteen army tents flapping and bellying in the breeze just outside the northern edge of Virginia City.

Gwen felt alone once more. It had been too much to hope for, that this stranger would help further.

''But I'll do this,'' Jordan went on, finding his hat and whacking the dust off on his leg. ''I'll stay with you until you report your trouble to the military, and I'll help you get that money in a safe place, where it won't blow away again. If I can help you hire a good escort to go with you, then I'll do that, too. But I can't be going with you.''

Somehow, in the back of Jordan's mind, he wondered just why he wouldn't go with this pretty girl. It might be an adventure, after all. He didn't quite know the answer. Did it have to do with what he'd seen in her eyes? He'd had plenty of women, and plenty of women were waiting for him, from the Dakotas to the Rio Grande. But this one was different. She attracted him strongly, but she wasn't one to love and leave, that was sure . . . He chuckled to himself as they mounted up and headed for town. Perhaps the reason he wanted to keep his distance was that she could shoot too well, and he wouldn't want her angry and coming after him.

Chapter 4

An hour later, they rode down onto Wallace Street and into Virginia City, as dusty, rickety, and downright stubborn a town as could be found in the West. The gold in the stream was nearly played out, but a few thousand miners still scrabbled about the hills, hunting through the sagebrush and cottonwood canyons for another lode. Uncounted hundreds of Chinese were crowded into dismal shanties on one side of town, where they lived a life that was secret, strange, and utterly puzzling as far as the Anglos were concerned. The ramshackle towns of Nevada and Alder Gulch farther down the Ruby River had once combined with Virginia City to fill the narrow valley with thirty-five thousand loud and hardworking, hard-drinking miners from every state in the union and nearly every continent on earth.

The boom days were gone now, but their memories remained. Gwen and Jordan came to the end of Wallace Street, the main thoroughfare, and dismounted. She led the mare, while he had the gelding in hand. They stared at the rows of one-story clapboard balloon frames decaying in the sunshine.

A few bore evidence of occupants, but more were vacant and falling down. Closer to the heart of town, it seemed that a coat of paint had been applied here and there, but not a human being was in sight. Dogs barked from alleyways, and the putrid smell of garbage piles there said that residents had been here not long before, but there were no people. Everything was shut and locked up tight, and the place seemed recently deserted.

"Like a ghost town," Jordan muttered, and looked from one side of the street to the other.

"Where've they all gone?" Gwen asked.

Then from a few hundred yards away, through back alleys and across flat roofs came the roar and shout of many hundreds of people. Jordan and Gwen looked at one another, wondering.

"Maybe a hanging," Gwen said, and knew she didn't want to go there.

The roar came to them again, echoing through the empty streets.

"Two hangings," Jordan replied.

The roar came again, and once again, then rose to a stormy pitch. Hundreds of voices were cheering for something.

"Horse race, maybe," Jordan said, and without further conversation, they turned the corner at Jackson Street and led the horses along. Now they could see, on the north end of Jackson Street, the dark and swirling mass of a mob.

"Something's happening," he said to Gwen. "You sure you want to go there?"

"I'll go if you will," she answered.

They went on, drawing closer to the surging mass, which was shouting and roaring fiercely. As they walked, they passed lines of hitched horses and scores of carts, carriages, and buggies, all parked in a jumbled crowd on both sides of the broad, rutted street.

"Well, that's what it is!" Jordan said, and paused as Gwen came to his side, stilling the nervous mare by putting a hand over its nose. "A prize fight!" Eighty yards away, up on a platform banded with ropes, two men, naked to the waist, were going at it.

Jordan took out his binoculars and looked at the fighters, one very short but superbly built and quick, and the other hefty, slow, but obviously strong.

"Must have just started or we'd have heard the crowd shouting sooner," Jordan said, handing the glasses to Gwen, who shook her head, refusing them.

"I've seen men fight before," she said. "It's not any nicer when they're doing it for money." She spoke quietly to the horse, which nuzzled against her shoulder.

Jordan stared through the binoculars for a moment longer, then scanned the crowd. "Soldiers there," he said. "No doubt Billy Buchanan'll be among 'em. Too bad we didn't come in sooner. I'd have bet with Billy . . . would've made a dollar, too. That boy always takes the wrong one—"

Jordan looked around to see Gwen moving a little back down the road, her mind on the horse she was leading.

"Where you going?" Jordan asked.

"Anywhere I don't have to watch or hear that."

A bell rang, and the crowd surging around the ring, hanging from false building fronts, swinging in trees, roared appreciation for its favorites. "Well, miss," Jordan said, "if I was lookin' for the commander of the soldiers here or for the sheriff or even the deputy sheriff or the marshal, I guess I'd start right there."

Gwen turned and looked at the crowd, her eyes distant, her hand on the horse's neck. She nodded to Jordan without speaking and turned the horse. As they came closer, the bell rang again, and Jordan saw that Gwen was looking down at the ground as she walked. For a girl who was as tough and independent as she was, she strangely had no stomach for a little organized bloodshed. He watched her as they walked until she looked up sharply at him.

"What?" she asked.

"Nothin'," he replied, but then began to say that there was something when he heard his name being shouted, loudly and raucously, joyously and tumultuously, above even the din of the hundreds who were following the boxers.

Jordan saw a giant of a cavalryman leap from out of the crowd and come charging, his great legs pounding up dust as he ran. "Jorrrrrdannn! You old hoss!"

"Billy! Eeeeyahoooo!"

Jordan whipped the hat from his head and ran with open arms for Sergeant Major Billy Buchanan, U.S. Seventh Cavalry, and the two friends rammed into each other. Jordan swung Billy off his feet, and that surprised Gwen, for Buchanan seemed half again as big as he. Then, in his turn, Buchanan picked up Jordan bodily, lifted him high over his head, and spun around clumsily, as though he would throw him through the nearby dry-goods store window. Gwen shrieked, and her hand went to her mouth.

Buchanan caught himself in midturn, recoiled like a spring, and stood staring at her, eyes wide with astonishment. He still held the laughing Jordan over his head as he said, "Wall, ah'll be . . . ah'll be hornswoggled . . . ah'll be a Yankee carpetbagger if you ain't done it this time, Jordan! Bless my Georgia picker's heart!"

Before Jordan could reply, Billy Buchanan brought him down as far as his waist, then let him fall the rest of the way. Buchanan, a slope-shouldered power of a man, strode forward, stepping over his friend, who was trying to get to his feet. As this giant came at Gwen, the grin on his face and the way he looked at her like a brother seeing a long-lost sister confused her emotion and her reason. Buchanan had short hair and was clean-shaven, with puffy red cheeks and a massive stomach that had seen less riding than garrison duty. He stopped a few feet away, and his eyes twinkled as he removed his hat and bowed graciously.

"Welcome to Virginia City, Mrs. Jordan. It ain't much, but then I don't figure you expect much from a wilderness like this, and surely you don't intend to stay very long."

In the next moment, with the noise of the prize fight rushing around them, Gwen Quinn and Billy Buchanan stared at each other, both completely at a loss for what to say next. Buchanan bobbed his head a little and asked. "Do yuh?" And he tried to keep smiling, but instead, his face turned vacant, and his eyes pried at Gwen for an answer.

"Do I what?" she asked. "I mean, what do you mean? I'm not Mrs. Jordan or Mrs. anyone else!"

She wasn't angry, just taken completely by surprise.

"You ain't?" Buchanan asked, and turned quickly to Jordan, now at the sergeant's shoulder, a smile on his face. Gwen was growing mildly annoyed at Jordan. This was on the verge of becoming a game, and she wanted no part of it.

Buchanan looked at Gwen and said, "More's the pity, then, for Grant Jordan. More's the pity, ma'am." He elbowed Jordan roughly and said, "Do the honors, then, old hoss; where's them Old Dominion gentilities?"

While Buchanan, hat in hand, grinned at Gwen, Jordan spoke. "Sergeant Major William Buchanan, ma'am, the federal army's very own Georgia cracker; a gent who never could give up the idea of havin' an officer tell him when to jump—Rebel or Yankee."

"At your service, ma'am," Buchanan bowed deeply again and put his battered blue army hat against his chest.

Jordan went on. "Sergeant Buchanan, Miss Gwen Quinn, a lady who'd like to talk with your commander right now."

"Now?" Buchanan asked, straightening up. "He's over watchin' the fight right now, and he don't take kindly to Southerners interruptin' his sport."

Jordan's face was serious as he said, "We got to speak to him, Billy. This lady's been in Injun trouble—a heap of it."

Buchanan suddenly became all business, his face sober, eyes hard. "I'll get the cap'n right away. Wait here, ma'am."

Buchanan lumbered off toward the noisy crowd, and Gwen glanced at Jordan, who said, "He's a good man to have along in a tight spot. I used to hunt buffalo with him just after the war, before he joined up with the cavalry. He was once a Rebel, too, but I guess he liked army life too much and couldn't stay out of fightin' somebody very long."

"I like him," Gwen said. Then she drifted into thought before she spoke again, slowly, and after a deep breath. "Mr. Jordan, will the army go out for . . . for Caleb and Silas? . . ." Her shoulders rose and fell with a sigh. "They should be laid to rest decently."

"Sure they will, ma'am," he replied, and stared down at his boots. "Sure they will."

A few moments later, Buchanan returned at the side of a slender, ramrod-straight captain, a man of about fifty whose hair was white under the dark-blue hat and whose bushy mustache was also pure white. Jordan thought the officer looked a little unsteady on his feet as he approached, but a stiff military bearing lent him an air of haughtiness and pride. The man stopped near them and took his hat off to Gwen, introducing himself as Captain William Rutledge. His voice slurred a bit as he spoke, and his cold blue eyes were watery.

"Now, then, young lady, my sergeant here says you've had some trouble with Indians." His voice was gruff, and his head tilted back as he spoke. "What's it all about?"

Before Gwen could speak, Jordan stepped next to her and said, "Captain, I think this is not a matter to be discussed outdoors. The lady has been through—"

"And just who are you, sir, to presume to interfere in military matters?" Rutledge's face turned red at what he considered impertinence—particularly since it came from some-one with a distinct southern drawl.

"He saved my life!" Gwen interrupted sharply. "If it wasn't for him—"

"Young lady," Rutledge said, and lifted a forefinger to stop her speaking. "Please be so kind as to let me get to the bottom of this with this fellow here, man to man." Rutledge directed himself at Jordan, who smelled a whiskey reek from even five feet away.

Jordan spoke first. "There's three dead white men down on the Beaverhead, and a burned stagecoach, too. I understand it's the federal army's job to prevent that sort of thing."

Rutledge's lip quivered as though his mind had frozen hearing about this disaster in his very own command region. He blustered and spat out flecks of foam as he struggled for words. "Hostiles!" was all that escaped. Then, in a burst of action, he spun to Buchanan, who jumped to attention as his superior blared, "Call out the company! Cancel all passes! Find the entire company right away! Find Lieutenant Wilkin-son and tell him to take—" He turned back to Jordan. "Just how many Indians were there? What tribe?"

Jordan thought a moment while Rutledge clenched and unclenched his fists at his sides, rocking on the balls of his feet. Then the hunter said, "Seemed less than fifteen in all. Couldn't tell the tribe, though they had some of the look of Crows, or—"

"Crows!" Rutledge snarled like a baited dog. "By gad! Crows! I knew it! Those slimy— Sergeant Buchanan, tell the lieutenant to take twenty men! When is that Crow band supposed to come in for government supplies?''

"Tomorrow afternoon, Cap'n."

Jordan tried to say he wasn't sure the hostiles were Crows, but Rutledge would hear none of it. The captain had already made up his mind which Indians had destroyed Gwen's coach. Rutledge had the look of a man possessed with a hunger for revenge as he sent Billy Buchanan off to gather the soldiers.

"Crows!" Rutledge said aloud to himself. "We'll teach those rascals a lesson they won't forget. They think they can come strolling in here high and mighty and command us to give them their treaty supplies after they kill innocent whites. . . . Well, they're not dealing with some pacifist, dreamy-eyed Quaker Indian agent now. . . ." Against the background sounds of the prize fight, he was ranting as if no one else were there. ". . . we'll put them in their place, the bloodthirsty—"

"Captain." Gwen spoke up, distracting him. "Captain, I urgently need the assistance of the military. My cousins were killed escorting me back to my father's mine in the Madisons, and I have no way to get back without protection."

Rutledge stuck out his chin as he asked, "And what do you expect from the United States Army, young lady?"

The roaring crowd nearly drowned out Gwen as she said, "Can you . . . can you send a patrol with me to guard my cargo . . . you see, I must get there immediately, or—"

But Rutledge was already shaking his head, eyes closed. "Young lady, young lady, what you ask is utterly impossible. Had I enough men to carry out my already cumbersome duties in this godforsaken wasteland, I'd only too gladly offer my services. But the fact is that I don't have enough soldiers even to protect the stage road south to the Beaverhead passes; if I were to order a detachment to accompany you . . . well, surely, young lady, you realize that everyone else would be knocking at my door the very next morning, begging me to send soldiers to protect them, too. Why not even Jess Clum, the freighter, asks me for that kind of protection for his wagons, and they're carrying a good deal of military supplies. Mr. Clum has the contract to see to our needs while we're stationed here in Virginia City, and he certainly is entitled to army escort. No, no . . .'' He shook his head and absently turned to eye the prize fight as the bell rang and the crowd shouted for the beginning of another round. Then he rubbed his hands together briskly. ''No, no, young lady, I regret I can't offer you my men, but I assure you that after I deal with this band of Crows coming in here in a day or so, you and everyone else traveling the highways will be perfectly safe from hostiles.''

Just then, someone called from the crowd. ''Well, look who's come to town!'' They turned to see a tall red-haired man step toward them. Gwen shuddered as she recognized Jess Clum.

He was someone she had no desire to see just then. Dressed in a three-piece pin-striped black suit and wearing a string tie and a beige derby, Clum looked the picture of prosperity. He was a powerful, influential person in the territory and had once been a partner of her father's up in Helena seven years earlier. They had owned a silver mine, with Clum financing it and Quinn in charge of mining operations. The mine had gone bust, but only after Clum and her father invested thousands of dollars, which were never recouped. For her father, the loss was devastating, coming only a year or two after the death of her mother in a typhoid epidemic. For Clum, the mine's demise meant a business disaster that took years to overcome. As a result of bankruptcy, the mine was sold to a Butte financier for a painfully low price, and the man had poured more money into it, turning it around and making it one of the territory's best silver producers, now worth millions.

Clum was even more furious with Tom Quinn when the mine's new owners made it a success. He blamed Quinn for the failure, and the two of them parted bitter enemies. That incident had been a serious blow to her father: Combined with the earlier loss of his son, the destruction of the farm in Shenandoah, and then the death of his beloved wife, it had very nearly broken him as a man. Tom Quinn had thrown himself into the Helena mine development with everything he had. When it went under, only Gwen's love kept him from complete despair, but the added humiliation of the new owners' making the mine a booming success had very nearly overwhelmed all Gwen's efforts to keep her father from giving up life itself.

When she saw Clum approaching, she did not give him the satisfaction of averting her eyes as he approached, a smug grin on his handsome face. He looked older than she remembered him. In the three years since last she saw Clum, he had grown a short mustache. He was about forty, well built, and in the prime of life. As he strolled casually toward the little group, he flitted an ebony cane with one hand and tipped his hat to Gwen with the other.

"It's been ever so long since Tom Quinn's little girl's been in Virginia City," he said, smiling, but with ice in his eyes. "Come to buy out the town to feed all those quartz miners up in the mountains, Miss Quinn?"

Gwen, for all her outward composure, was at a loss for words. But Rutledge spoke up, saying, "Jess, this young lady has met tragic circumstances. Crows destroyed a stage she hired and killed her companions down on the Beaverhead!"

"Crows!" Clum looked angry, genuinely troubled by this news as he said to the captain, "I knew it was the Crows from the beginning! I'm sure they're the ones who cut off the wagon convoys going into the Madisons last month." He turned to Gwen. "I do believe those wagons were headed for the Quinn mine, too, were they not?"

Gwen nodded and looked away from Clum, whose eyes were hard and steely blue.

"Most unfortunate," Clum said, and flicked the air with his cane again. "It seems all your father's mining enterprises are doomed to meet with bad luck—"

"Don't you say that!" Gwen burst out. "You have no right—" She restrained herself when she realized how much he would enjoy seeing Tom Quinn's daughter break down and scream at him in public.

"Now, now, Miss Quinn . . ." Rutledge began, glancing over his shoulder as the crowd at the boxing match shouted again for the fighters. "My word, now," Rutledge mumbled, obviously anxious not to miss the fight. Then he said to Gwen in a stiff, formal tone, "Miss Quinn, be assured that the army will do everything in its power to assist you in this matter . . . short of providing an armed escort, of course, as I said. And we'll investigate the hostilities and bring to justice the dastardly villains who perpetrated this crime."

"Well said, Captain!" Clum exclaimed. "I'm sure you'll deal harshly with the Crows coming to town! Teach them a lesson once and for all! It's the only way we'll be safe!"

"Exactly!" Rutledge slapped his hands together. "We'll have peace—" The crowd roared again, and Rutledge turned to look.

"Captain," Clum said, and put his hand familiarly on the officer's arm, "this is quite a fight, eh? I wonder who'll take the glory. Two men, perfectly matched—"

At that, Jordan stepped forward so that he bumped Clum's shoulder, his face close enough to the captain's so that the smell of drink on the officer's breath was repulsive. "Is this fight more important than Miss Quinn's loss?" He had now shouldered Clum out of the way, feeling reckless and mean. Clum stepped back and twirled his cane, a grin creeping over his face.

Rutledge was taken a little aback. He didn't like Jordan's pushiness one bit, but he could not deny the man's point.

"All will be in order, sir," Rutledge said, and stuck out his chest, his lower lip quivering again in indignation. "Without interference from the likes of you!"

"You'll need my interference if you want to find that stage," Jordan said, barely restraining his anger. "I'll guide a detachment down there right away—"

"Will you now?" Rutledge was florid, and he stepped back, sneering, "Tell me, then, fellow, just how many men should I send? And should they remain out long? Would you like to specify arms and supplies as well, or do you think that the United States Army might just be able to fend for itself without your commands?"

Jordan stared at Rutledge, sensing Clum snickering nearby. "I guess if the army doesn't know what to do by now, Captain, those Indians'll make fools of you."

Rutledge was on the brink of blowing up, his teeth virtually chattering, but the mob behind him let out a mighty shout, distracting him again and offering Jess Clum the opportunity to step in and say, when the roar died down, "You and I have a wager on this, Captain, and I don't want to miss the fun." He put his arm on the officer's shoulders and said, "You promised you wouldn't let anything spoil your sport today."

Rutledge composed himself. Jordan, who was now calm and self-possessed, stared at Clum, who did not look back. Pouting, Rutledge told Gwen to appear at his headquarters at the foot of Cover Street later that afternoon, and then she could file a full report of the attack. In the meantime, he said, a detachment under Lieutenant Wilkinson would leave for the site of ambush and recover the bodies of her "unfortunate companions." The aging officer gave Jordan a scathing look and said, "Since you show such interest in this young lady, I'll accept your offer to guide my men. I'm unable to accompany you because my duties require me to be here when the Crows come in for their supplies. The patrol will come back immediately—no pursuit will be permitted. We'll need every man back here tomorrow."

He said to Gwen, who was downcast, "You have my sympathies. But until this country is rid of these red-skinned vermin . . . Well, young lady, I must be about my business. I trust you are in good hands with this . . . ah, Southern gentleman." He forced a tight smile and turned away, vanishing into the crowd.

With bitter anger, Jordan watched him go. "Pompous Yankee—" Then he cut himself off as he heard Gwen sob.

"Oh, I'm sorry," she said, turning her face to the neck of the mare.

He came close to her, and in a moment, when the crowd noise abated, he said, "We'll get you through this. Come on, we'll find a place for you to stay."

Together, they led their horses back down the empty street with the savage rumbling of the mob loud and eager behind them. Gwen's head was down. She faced again the difficult task of getting the payroll and new supplies through dangerous country to the mine. Jordan felt sympathy for her, and he also felt a different uneasiness within himself. He had many close friends among the Crows, and he wondered just what that drunken Captain Rutledge had in mind when the expected party from that tribe arrived at Virginia City. Whatever it might be, Jordan knew Captain Rutledge planned serious trouble for the Crows.

Jordan's eyes also were on the ground as they walked. For a man who wanted only to mosey northward and locate good hunting grounds and a camp to hole up in for the winter, he was finding life suddenly damn complicated!

Chapter 5

They walked for a while without talking, leading the horses as they went. Jordan thought again how despondent this place looked. He knew Virginia City had once cherished hopes of becoming the territorial capital of Montana, but two years ago, Helena, ninety miles north, had been selected by the legislature, deeply disappointing the people of this town. Now, with the placers yielding but a little gold to only the dogged Chinese, there was nothing much left to keep anyone here, and more than half the buildings were unoccupied. Many still carried ambitious names—the Chicago House, the Miner's Delight, the Gilded Cage—and all held faint memories of delirious nights, boisterous celebration, gambling, devastating losses, costly love, and killings.

It was here and down in Bannack that the vigilantes had organized with a vengeance in 1863 and wiped out a large gang of murderous highwaymen who called themselves the "Innocents." In six savage weeks that winter, the men of the mining camps formed miner's courts and tried and summarily hanged twenty-two of the worst villains for crimes ranging from jumping claims to murder. Others were banished, and many of the rest were frightened out of the country. The vigilantes also hanged the leader of the Innocents, the ruthless Henry Plummer, whose cronies had elected him sheriff of Bannack. Vigilance committee activity had lessened by 1865, when statutory law took hold, but there were vigilante hangings as late as 1870. Jordan himself had seen one such hanging up in Helena; he'd been part of a crowd of a thousand persons who gathered in the courthouse square to see two hoodlums strung up. He never wanted to see a hanging again.

Jordan's thoughts returned to the present, and he looked closely at Gwen, saw the lovely face, the sad, sad eyes, and he was moved to say, "You know, things never seem quite as bad once you've put a little distance between yourself and them."

She did not look up, and he tried again. "I mean, no matter what happens, you have to go on. You have to lift up your head and . . . and, well. . . you have to go on." He knew his words were shallow, but he had to say something. She looked over at him and then back at the ground.

"Now I've no meanin' to make light of anythin', Miss Quinn, but I'd say that you're the kind can come through adversity with your head high . . . or, not exactly high, or proud, like, but . . . ah . . ."

He stopped, and so did she, and she looked at him again, her eyes shining with tears. Jordan shook his head and took off his hat.

"Ma'am," he said, and ran his hand through his hair. "Ma'am, I don't know what in thunder I'm talkin' about, and I hope you'll forgive me for goin' on about what I don't . . ."

He slapped the hat back on his head, pursed his lips, and stared hard at the ground.

Gwen stepped toward him and said, "You're very nice, Mr. Jordan. And I . . . I don't know what to say either."

They began to walk again, heads down, the horses plodding behind. After a few moments, Gwen looked up to see they were at the end of Broadway, facing a sparse straggle of tiny shacks at the base of rolling hills beyond that were like swells on a sea after a storm. They both stopped, gazing out at the bracken and sagebrush crowding in the edge of town.

Still not speaking, they turned left down Cover Street, heading toward Ruby Creek, where the Chinese at the placers were sluicing water and silt into slurries that showed so little gold that ten years ago it would have been considered less than worthless. A self-respecting placer miner who was after sudden wealth would have packed his gear and headed out if he did as poorly as these Chinese. In those boom days, there was always word of another bonanza somewhere over the next mountain.

They stood at the end of Cover Street, watching straw-hatted coolies shoveling soil into muddy water slowly seeping along the sluice framework. Here the road turned northward, downstream, past the remains of smaller mining communities— Alder, Laurin, Ruby, Junction City, Adobetown, Nevada City, and Central City, most of them ghost towns long ago. In a flat area on their right were two dozen tents for the soldiers who were temporarily stationed here. From where Gwen and Jordan stood, looking down the creek, it seemed a giant hog had rooted up the soil and riven rocks and slope drift into a dirty furrow that ran away into the hills. Actually, this was the hurried work of thousands of placer miners. The entire stretch of Ruby Creek looked like that, and now it was played out, abandoned.

Jordan had nothing to say to Gwen, but he could not take leave of her even though they had shared nothing more than a quick, fiery memory of yesterday's danger and a slow, dusty walk through the streets of Virginia City. In the background, over the hiss and clatter of water running down from a dam just above the town, they heard the shouting of the crowd at the fight.

"What will you do now?" Gwen asked, not looking at him, but rather out at the brown and dingy placer works that gutted the stream.

"Maybe I can find out from Billy Buchanan about some men you can depend on."

She nodded. "I'd appreciate that, Mr. Jordan."

"Grant."

She smiled again. Then she went back to the duffel bag hanging from the mare and untied it, taking out the strongbox. Jordan looked around quickly and saw no one was close enough to see it. But still he was anxious. "I don't think you should show that box," he said, and stepped toward her.

Gwen held it out to him. "There's ten thousand dollars in there," she said. "I'd like to give you a thousand of it. I wish it could be more, but you see, we need the rest—"

Jordan pushed the box back at her. "Thank you, ma'am. But I think you need that thousand. Where I'm goin' this winter I won't need money, and if I had it along, I'd likely lose it or gamble it or give it to someone who didn't deserve it—"

"Really, I must insist—"

"No. I mean it. I don't want that money . . . not at all. Your pa can use it better than I ever could." Then he considered a moment before saying, "Well, now, it is possible that there's a way you might repay me. . . ."

"Yes?"

"The Chicago House claims the best cookin' in the Rockies. It's the only thing this town's good for now, I'd wager, but tourists to Yellowstone Park say it's good, and where I'm goin', there won't be anything like it—they claim to favor a

place called Delmonico's back East in New York, and I'd
like to see just what it's like to eat food cooked like they do
in New York.''

Gwen looked puzzled.

''You want to take me to dinner? I'm afraid I wouldn't—''

''No, you take me! Right now! Spendin' greenbacks on
that kind of food seems frivolous to me, but eatin' it, well,
that's another thing. I wouldn't feel the least squeamish about
eatin' it. We have to go now, though, before Buchanan looks
me up, since I'm going out with his patrol.''

Gwen thought about that a moment and found herself
welling with good feeling for this buffalo hunter who had
contrived once again to cheer her up despite everything. She
was grateful for that.

She put the strongbox in a satchel on the packhorse as she
said, ''Let's go and have a meal you can remember when
you're up north snowed inside an Indian wigwam this winter.''

Jordan knew Gwen's heart would not be in for sociable
dining at that moment, but he figured it would do her good.
Besides, he thought as they left for the Chicago House, he
wouldn't mind being in her company a little longer.

A short while later, they came to the hotel with an impos-
ing name but a forlorn outer appearance. The building was
two stories high, so it did not need the square-rigged false
front that so many lesser western frameworks employed to
suggest something more than a structure really was. But those
two stories were weary ones, in need of paint and repair
work. The faded sign said ''Chicago House'' in rusty red
lettering, but that was all to suggest it was a hotel.

Gwen and Jordan hitched the horses to the rail and went up
the wooden steps to the porch. But they were disappointed.
The doors were closed and padlocked. At the window hung a
sign: ''Gone to the fight. Open after Mullady dines on canvas.''

The fight was still under way at least an hour after it had begun. Gwen looked at the crowd clogging the far end of the street like a mass of ants.

"Well, ma'am, looks like we'll have to wait till Mullady eats canvas before we can eat a steak Delmonico style." He stepped down to the street. "We should get these horses grained and put up. I'll get a fresh mount from the army when I ride out with them. You can buy me dinner when I come back. What are you going to do now?"

Gwen thought of all she would have to do before she could resume her journey. "I'll go to the Wells Fargo office and try to hire another stagecoach. It's the fastest way, faster than going by freight wagon. I'll have to order supplies and get more dynamite from the mining store. Then . . ." The army report; arranging for men to escort her; getting an undertaker to inter her cousins . . . She felt as though she were up against a brick wall. The hissing, grumbling, screaming mass of people at the prize fight throbbed within her tired mind.

Jordan sensed the weight on her and said, "Look, I'll get Billy Buchanan to turn up a few boys you can trust, and when I get back from goin' with him to the Beaverhead, I'll help you sort everything out."

"Thank you, Grant. Having the men will be a relief, but I intend to arrange everything else right away. I've got no time to lose, and already I'm later than I should be." In a few words, she told him more about her predicament, saying that her father's men had to be paid, telling of the Salt Lake syndicate that was after possession of the mine. He understood the gravity of her position, and once more he wondered why he was letting himself get dragged deeper into her affairs.

They parted company after that—she going to the supply stores and the Wells Fargo office, he heading down the street to the fight, where Buchanan would be rounding up his soldiers. Jordan also was interested in seeing whether this Mullady really would dine on canvas.

He found Buchanan there with twenty grumbling soldiers all angry at having to go out after hostiles while the prize fight was going on. Buchanan was not very enthusiastic, either, and if it had not been for having met Gwen Quinn, he might have been less professional in rousting out the detachment. Lieutenant Wilkinson was not there yet, but Buchanan had his charges loosely assembled, waiting for him where they could see the bare-knuckled battle up in the ring. Standing with the soldiers, Jordan watched the bigger fighter, Mullady, plod stubbornly after his quicker, lighter opponent, named "Con" Mathews. Both men were bloody and red-faced, both walking in with heads down, still strong even though the fight had been going on for nearly two hours and more than a hundred rounds.

For all the difference in size between the two men, it seemed an even match. Jordan found himself instinctively moving with the fighters, just as every man there was swaying and bobbing in rhythm with the boxers. For a while, Jordan forgot about Indians, about his hunger, and even about Gwen Quinn. Then they were joined by Lieutenant Wilkinson, a boyish, dark-haired New Englander with a curling mustache and a weak chin. It was almost an hour later when the soldiers were armed and mounted up, heading out to the Ruby Range in a column of twos. As the troopers moved slowly over the first ridge, each man was craning his neck to look back at the distant fight. Billy Buchanan and Jordan sat their horses on a knoll, watching the distant hubbub far below. Lieutenant Wilkinson was at the head of the column, and Buchanan was assigned to Jordan to plan out the route of the patrol. But before they had discussed the route, Buchanan said, "It's over! They're breakin' up!"

Sure enough, the mass of ants scattered suddenly, pouring

down Jackson Street, no doubt heading for the saloons to pay off debts or to be paid off. The fight had gone on for three brutal hours.

"Guess you wish you knew who won, eh, Billy?" Jordan asked.

"Don't worry about that. I will. Just wait." Buchanan strained as though listening for something. By now, the other soldiers were reluctantly moving out of sight of town, the column snaking down the opposite slope.

Then two spaced shots came from the town, a signal to Buchanan, who yanked off his hat and slapped his thigh, yahooing that he was forty dollars richer because Mullady had won! But suddenly there came four spaced shots, and that befuddled the sergeant and turned every head in the patrol.

"What the hell? . . ." Buchanan grunted. "That means Con won, too. . . . What the hell?"

"A draw," Jordan said with a grin. "They were matched too well, Billy. You never could pick a winner."

Once the prize fight was finished and Virginia City returned to normal, Gwen could get about her business. Her first stop, at the Wells Fargo office, was a bad start. She was told there that no stagecoaches would be available for hire until the Indian trouble was over. The company was running only its regular route north to Helena and down to Salt Lake City, and there were extra guards on the run to protect the stages. The clerk at the office told Gwen that she likely could hire an old coach from Horace Greenfield over in the Madison River valley on the east side of the Rubys. Greenfield ran a feeder line between Bozeman in the north and Virginia City. He leased coaches to tourists heading for Yellowstone National Park ninety miles south.

Gwen was despondent that no Wells Fargo stage was available, but she went on to order another two hundred pounds of dynamite and arranged for mining equipment needed to break open the rock face blocking access to the rich vein of gold her father was sure lay at the base of Koch Peak. She knew what must be done. The supplies had to be shipped by freight wagon to Greenfield's independent stage station, there to be transferred to a fast stage—if one was available. If no stage could be hired, then she would have no other choice but to transport everything by slow-moving wagon. That meant a delay of more than a week in getting the payroll to the mine, and that week might mean everything, might mean the work would be abandoned because the miners had walked out. These thoughts caused deep anxiety, but Gwen would do whatever she must to get the payroll through, even if it meant taking a horse through the mountains alone, leaving the wagon and its guards to come on behind. For a moment, she wished Grant Jordan would change his mind and go with her—then braving the mountains would not be so fearful. But first there was the problem of finding a wagon and teamsters to get the supplies and dynamite the first stage to the Madison Valley.

One alternative would be to go to the freight-line owner, Jess Clum, and ask to hire one of his wagons and men. But that thought repelled her instantly, and she discarded it. To give Clum the opportunity to refuse her request at this critical moment would be an indignity Gwen could not bear. So she was grateful an hour later when the mining supply firm offered a wagon and two teamsters to take the goods to the Madison Valley. The firm owner was an old friend of her father's, and he agreed to help Gwen, but as for sending the men and wagon an additional forty miles through badlands to the mine, that was too dangerous. The man told her that his own convoys heading up to Quinn's mine were the ones that had been attacked a month earlier, and his men had barely escaped with their lives, several being badly wounded.

Now Gwen had the first part of her work arranged. The problem now was to get the money—which was in a safe at the Wells Fargo office—and the cargo the rest of the way. As she walked to the Chicago House, she passed another crowd—this one with some women—filling a vacant lot and sprawling into the street. Her mind was on other matters as she pushed through, but she chanced to look up at the center of attention and saw a robust, purple-faced orator standing on the back of a wagon, intoning deep and sonorous words to the crowd.

This was a traveling preacher, and his sermon was the usual fare of anecdote and loosely quoted Scripture, but the crowd seemed in a favorable mood to listen to him. After the excitement of the fight and the unfruitfulness of the betting, the mob was willing enough to hear this parson remind them of their sins and warn them to repent before it was too late.

Weaving through the crowd was slow work, and Gwen found herself listening to more of the sermon than she had intended. The fellow was a good speaker, and he told a colorful story about the dream that set him off preaching on the frontier.

Gwen was nearly out of the press of people when the parson said, "I had been many, many hours in prayer, my friends, attempting to comprehend the call of the Lord. Never has any believer struggled harder with his destiny than I did on that night so long ago when I prayed for the light to shine upon my unworthy eyes. At last, overcome by physical and mental exhaustion, I fell into deep slumber and dreamed." He paused for effect. The crowd was quiet now, listening closely. Gwen, too, lingered, always fascinated by the glazed eyes and guilty faces at such sermons.

"My friends, in that dream on that glorious night, I saw the figure of an angel dressed in shining raiment descend from silvery clouds. This vision pointed out to me three fiery letters engraved upon that pearly cloud. Those letters were *G P C*; and, friends, it was with amazement and in humble benediction that I heard this angel's voice say softly, like the ringing of a silvery bell, 'Follow these.' And, my friends, I understood immediately what these sacred letters meant. I understood, in that divine moment of my unworthy life, just what those three letters spelled out—'' After savoring his pregnant pause, he said slowly, with a deep voice: '' 'Go preach Christ!' ''

The preacher bowed his head, hands tight on the rostrum before him. The crowd hung on his oration, suspended, until an old, cracked voice spoke from the back of the crowd. ''You sure, preacher, it didn't mean 'Go pick cotton'?''

A whoop went up from the audience, and the spell was broken. Only the more demure women tried to restrain their laughter. The minister was furious and even more purple now as he searched the audience for the culprit.

''Laugh! Go on and laugh, sinners! But you'll be shoveling hot coals and brimstone when the day of judgment comes!'' Then he sent some of his own fire and brimstone sparking among the listeners, and those few who did not drift off for home or for the saloons were the ones whose hearts were deeply troubled. Gwen made it through the crowd, and she thought about that impertinent voice, thought she recognized it from somewhere.

Just as she reached the edge of the crowd, she saw an old man in a fringed buckskin shirt sitting on an overturned barrel. Amos Meeker! So he was the heckler! In his tattered Levi overalls and stovepipe hat with the brim turned down so it looked like a cone, Amos looked just as he had five years ago when she last saw him. Lying at his side was old Misty, the floppy-eared coonhound that followed him everywhere.

''Amos!'' she shouted, and ran for him.

Meeker cackled and rose from the barrel, though his bent

legs stayed bent as if he were still sitting. He took the pipe from his toothless mouth and whooped as they hugged one another. He was slender, but his arms felt strong, his body wiry and durable.

"Easy, easy there, Missy Quinn. Don't whirl me too hard or you'll have to fetch an arm or leg from the street!" He chuckled and said, "My, you growed since I last saw you, girlie! An' you look better'n your pappy ever did! Yep!" He stood back and stuck the pipe in his mouth as he said, "Look jest like that mother o' your'n. The image! Ain't that so, Misty?"

He looked down at the sleepy brown hound, which gave an imperceptible move of his tail and yawned. Gwen knelt to give the dog a rough petting and felt good at seeing these two again. Meeker had worked for her father as a shooter—an explosives man—up at the Helena mine, but he was also once known as the finest stagecoach driver in the Rockies. Eight years ago, he quit driving to become a gold hunter throughout Idaho, Montana, and Colorado. He had been loyal to her father right to the end of the Helena mine bankruptcy, but he had needed work and had gone off to Colorado to hunt gold.

Gwen invited Meeker to join her at the hotel for the dinner she had promised Grant Jordan. With Misty munching scraps under the table, she poured out her troubles to the old man.

He ate hungrily and afterward sipped a beer, thinking hard about all she had told him.

"Well, what do you think?" she asked at last, leaning forward in her chair. Around them, the hotel's regular customers had long before departed, and a restless waiter was watching them from the kitchen door. The restaurant was shabby but still had the threadbare trappings of former prosperity. As Jordan had said, the food was excellent. Outside, it was dark, and candles and coal-oil lamps cast a warm, yellow glow over the white tablecloth and the light-green dress Gwen had borrowed from the daughter of the mining supply company proprietor.

He said finally, "Well, Missy Quinn, it looks like you an' yer pa's in a fix. Reckon I could find the time to lend you a helpin' hand. I'll drive the stage from Greenfield's to the mine—"

Before he could finish, she was up and hugging him. "Oh, Amos! Amos! Oh, Amos, thank you! I know everything will be all right now!"

From under the table, Misty woofed and let his head thunk back down onto his paws once more. Meeker recovered himself and returned to his beer, while Gwen began to make plans, mapping out their route from the stage stop on the Madison southward to the mine. Amos filled and lit his pipe, not saying a word until she had talked herself out.

The old-timer puffed quietly for a while before speaking. Then he said, "I ain't willin' to bet Horace Greenfield will have a stage on hand just when you want it," and Gwen felt tenseness coming on again. "But if he don't, then it just so happens that I know a way to get around that problem." He muttered, almost to himself, saying, "Might be the best way to do it . . . 'cause if she can't outrun them redskins, no Greenfield rig'll do it. It's risky. If we run into trouble, I might lose her. . . . Wouldn't care about Greenfield's rig much. Course drivin' Greenfield's I ain't so sure we could come out with our hair. . . . Up them hills . . . might be best to go the nat'ral bridge cross the gorge. . . . Not likely the Injuns'd look fer us that direction. . . ."

"Amos?" Gwen ventured. "Amos . . . mind letting me in on what you're thinking?"

"Eh? Yep . . ." He sat up in his chair. "Well, can't say I know myself, yet. But you'll know soon enough, Missy Quinn. I got some thinkin' to do afore we cut for your pa's mine. First we go to Greenfield's an' see what he's got to offer." He spoke to himself again. "One thing Greenfield's got is good horseflesh. That boy'll have what we need to haul the rig, that's sure. Two span'll do . . . three'd be faster, but too much for them twisty roads . . . don't want to go over a cliff. . . ."

Without questioning him further, Gwen finished her coffee—Delmonico's style and price—and listened to old Amos talk to himself. She caught enough to realize he was thinking of an alternate route to the mine, one he thought would likely be out of the way of the hostiles. It was dangerous, she understood, but she trusted this man implicitly.

Meeker muttered on to himself, pipe staying barely lit only by an occasional absent puff. Gwen distracted herself by feeding old Misty some sweet roll and pointedly ignored the annoyed waiter, who wished they were gone. Through it all, she kept hearing Meeker refer fondly to some "she" they could apparently count on heavily in the attempt to outrun the Indians. At last, Gwen had to ask, "Amos, who?"

"What?" He stirred a little, one eyebrow cocking, the pipe jutting up.

"Who's she?"

"Who's who, girl? Speak up, will you? I can't hear as good as I used to, and I don't recall things as good as some'd like me to. Who? Was you talkin' about somebody? What?"

"Not me," Gwen said, and ran her finger around the rim of her cup. "You. You were talking about some lady who'll help us."

"Lady?" A grin broadened the wrinkled, weathered face, and he said, "Lady? You could say that, though she's a jaded one after all these years—"

"Amos! I don't want to know anything about her past. It's no matter to me. I've lived around mining towns all these years, and I've seen her kind before—"

Meeker cackled again, high and delightedly. He shook his

head and looked under the table at the hound. "Missy Quinn'll sure think Arabella's a lady, won't she, Misty? Yes, indeed!" He looked back at Gwen, his eyes twinkling with his secret. "Indeed you will, Missy Quinn, if Arabella's called upon to get us through. Indeed you will."

"Who's Arabella, then?"

"That's my secret," Meeker said, puffing his pipe alive again. "And you won't know it 'less you have to. She's been my secret for nigh on eight year now, and she'll stay a secret if Horace Greenfield can fix us up with a decent rig." He jerked his head once as though resolving to go ahead with something, then said, "Yep, she's my secret, but for Tom Quinn and you, missy, I'll risk her."

With that, Meeker rose, Gwen left some money and followed, and Misty padded after them—in his mouth was Meeker's battered old coachman's topper, which would have been left behind and lost long ago had Misty not been used to his master's forgetful ways.

They put on jackets and stepped out into the cool, refreshing night. Stars were bright, and the hills surrounding Virginia City were black swelling mounds against the sky. Near them an oil lamp glowed at the hotel door, and down the street the clink of honky-tonk pianos lent cheer to the darkness.

Meeker breathed in the air, and Gwen came to his side. "Amos, do you think we'll get through?" she asked softly.

His pipe glowed as he pulled at it, sending gray and yellowish smoke drifting at the oil light. He leaned down to take his hat from Misty and chucked the dog under the floppy jowls. Then he said, without looking up at her, "If you don't think we can make it, then you shouldn't try."

The awesome responsibility of what she was doing engulfed Gwen just then. She had already seen two cousins killed. Did she have the right to put Amos in danger—Amos and whoever else agreed to go along for hire? She did not know the answer to that when she said, "I don't know if we can make it, Amos. I don't know at all. But . . . whatever might happen, I'm going, and I'm going if I have to go alone! If you want to change your mind—"

Amos put his hand on her arm, looked her in the eyes, and nodded slowly. "I feel the way you do, missy. I don't know if we can make it, either."

Across those dark mountains, twenty hard miles to the southwest, Grant Jordan lay with his head on his saddle, an army-issue blanket covering his body against the cold. He listened to the wind and the coyotes up in the hills. It was another night without a campfire because the hostiles might slip up on their camp before dawn. There was no sense making the patrol easy targets by firelight.

They had ridden steadily after leaving Virginia City that afternoon, making five miles an hour over a different, easier road than Jordan had used to get to the town. Nearby, in the darkness, lay Buchanan and a few others. Jordan's night eyes picked out the lone sentry walking on the perimeter of the camp.

He turned on his side, the ground stiff and painful under his slicker, which was spread beneath him. How he longed to sleep in a hotel tonight—even in a hayloft, for that matter. Anywhere but out here above the Beaverhead, near the ravine where the stagecoach had been ambushed. Perhaps it was more than the hard ground that kept him awake. Perhaps it was also the thoughts tumbling in his mind that made sleep difficult—thoughts of the three dead men at the destroyed stage. And thoughts about what Gwen Quinn was going to do tomorrow.

It was sure she would never need an undertaker to inter her cousins. They were too mangled by the explosion even to take back to town, as was the stage driver. Their bodies were buried in the gulch, the soldiers sickened by their work even though they were professionals, experienced with death. But the sight of a disfigured body is never really forgotten, and Jordan sensed the anger these men bore for Indians. Thinking they were Crows, the troopers and Lieutenant Wilkinson had muttered about what they would like to see happen to the Crows coming into Virginia City soon. That bothered Jordan almost as much as Gwen Quinn's predicament.

He had friends among the Crows, and he didn't like the looks of Captain Rutledge or this pipsqueak young lieutenant who was second in command. The lieutenant knew his business well enough; Jordan could tell this by the way he investigated the ambush site and saw that the attackers had numbered about fourteen and read the blood sign right, seeing that at least three had been shot. But the lieutenant was too eager, too anxious to prove himself. Maybe any young fellow under an officer like Rutledge would have trouble coming out well. Drunks in command were bad enough to handle, but if Buchanan's story of Rutledge's career was true—and surely it was—then the captain was a dangerous superior to buck or to follow.

Officers like Captain Rutledge got men unnecessarily killed and gave the army a bad name—no matter whose army they were in. Jordan had seen a few of his kind fighting in the Rebel cause, too. A man had to watch them closely and see when they were about to explode. . . .

Jordan recalled Buchanan's words about Rutledge: "Mighta made a good officer if he hadn't spent the war up in Fort Snelling, freezin' his butt off and commandin' niggers who'd been slaves the week before. That got his goat. Rutledge knows the book, and he goes by it, but he never got a field command to bring him recognition, and after the war, he was demoted from major to captain, like a lot of other career men, because no peacetime army needs a lot of generals, and all the generals were busted down to colonel, and I even know of a general who fought as a scout down in Arizona with the rank of sergeant. . . . Anyhow, this Rutledge has missed every fight an' war that ever was, an' he's still missin' 'em.

"Missed the big war because he was a garrison commander; missed the Indian wars in the late sixties because he was back East behind a desk; missed Crook and Sheridan fightin' with the Sioux and Cheyenne, and that danged bug-tit is sorrier than a jilted bride that he didn't get a chance to go under with Custer an' half the Seventh up on the Little Big Horn last year! Believe me, Jordan, this man has Yankee blue for blood but the devil's own mother for a patron saint. He can't get into a fight no way, and ever since his wife ran off and left him last year, he's been drinkin' Valley Tan like it comes from the well.

"I say if I was a Crow comin' into Virginia City and I knew about Captain Willie Rutledge, I'd turn my feathers 'round and head east for the Yellowstone agency instead!

"And what's more, the captain's got a newfangled Gatlin' gun. Shoots faster'n I can talk, it does. Yes, suh, Johnny Reb, this hoss don't like the smell of what's comin', an' I don't mind much shootin' an Injun now an' then, but I like 'em to know I'm gunnin' for 'em first!"

Buchanan had gone on like that, as they lay near each other in their blankets, until he fell asleep only a few minutes ago. Or Jordan thought he was asleep, but then the twangy Georgia voice spoke up. "An' what's more, that bug-tit is sorer'n hell that he ain't in on the fightin' with the Nez Percé! Sorer'n hell that he's just a mountain or two away from some real glory shootin' up peaceable Injuns that don't cotton to no government reservation!"

Jordan said, "Those Nez Percé are whippin' everything the army's sent after them, I hear."

"You're right there," Buchanan said, and put his head

down. "An' that's why Rutledge is jest prayin' they cut through this country on their run to Canada. Like I said, he's got that there Gatlin' gun."

"It doesn't shoot faster'n you talk, Billy."

"Almost. But not as straight."

They lay quiet again. The sentry's boots cracked over twigs as he walked. A man snored here; one muttered to himself there. A coyote howled, and Jordan's saddle leather creaked as he turned onto his back. He wished he could get to sleep. He was tired enough, but his mind was too busy, too full of troubles—other people's troubles, for sure, but he had the feeling they were fast becoming his own, whether he liked it or not.

Chapter 6

AT eleven o'clock of the next day, Gwen was in the mining store, scheduling the departure of a wagonload of mining supplies for that afternoon. She would wait for Grant Jordan to return with the army patrol and get his help in rounding up a few likely men to go with her. She planned to leave the next day for Greenfield's stage station on the Madison. Gwen bid good day to the clerk at the supply store and stepped out the door onto the boardwalk. She looked up to see a rider galloping through town, shouting that the Crow Indians had arrived and were camping down the gulch. Many men elbowed each other and joked that there would be a lively time to come when Captain Rutledge went out to treat with the redskins. Gwen heard men laying odds on whether there would be gunplay or not. Most bet there would be.

But that was not her concern now. She had to go to the hotel, meet Amos Meeker, and get a message to the army camp, asking Jordan to come to the Chicago House when he got back. Her eyes were down as she walked—she again wore her jeans, boots, flannel shirt, and a new tan Stetson she had bought that morning—so she did not notice a man step in front of her. Surprised, she bumped into him before she could stop, and he gripped her by the arms, drawing her to him.

It was Jess Clum.

"Get your hands off me!" She struggled to free herself.

Clum smiled sweetly and said, "Don't be that way, Miss Quinn. Hold on. I just want to talk to you—"

"Then do your talking at a distance!" She yanked one arm free, but he held the other tightly. "I said, let go!" Gwen stamped her heel hard on his instep, and he gasped, jumping back and hopping a bit. Miners standing at the entrance to the Wells Fargo office chuckled and tossed teasing remarks at Clum, who glared at them and then at Gwen.

"You Quinns are all the same . . ." he began through clenched teeth, then cut himself off and took a deep breath, straightening up and wiggling his sore foot as he did so. "Now you listen, little lady. You don't know what kind of trouble you're getting yourself into. I'm only saying this because Tom was a partner once—"

"You don't owe us anything!"

Clum gave a sly grin, a knowing look that made Gwen feel a crawling chill under her skin. "I surely don't, that's true. But I hate to see a nice young thing like you put her life in danger. And that's what you'll be doing if you try to go through the mountains next week."

"Not next week, tomorrow!" Gwen said quickly, immediately wishing she had not said it, wishing she had kept her movements secret.

Clum smiled again. "And you know Horace Greenfield hasn't got a stage to hire. All those tourists to Yellowstone have cleaned him out."

Clum obviously had been asking around, and he knew a lot, she thought. What was his interest in all this? She listened, her eyes insolent and haughty, as he said, "You can't outrun Indians in a freight wagon, Miss Quinn. And they'll be looking for stray wagons here and there to hit. Listen to me! You're on a fool's errand!''

"I'll be the judge of that."

He nodded his head, then took off his derby. "You're a mite young to know so much, aren't you? Miner's daughters don't get that wordly from flirting with miner's employees. Come to your senses! You won't get through—"

Gwen shoved past him. "Get out of my way!"

He grabbed her roughly by the arm again and started to yank her back, but she went with the force of the pull and hit him hard on the ear with her open hand. Clum swore, dropped his ebony cane, and staggered back, while the men standing nearby hooted and laughed. He came at her then, and Gwen kicked savagely, missing but causing him to move aside. Clum was steaming with fury now, and he raised his hands to grab her, but he reeled from a stinging blow to the side of his head that sent him sprawling off the boardwalk and into the dusty street, where nervous horses hitched nearby whinnied and shied to get out of his way as he rolled.

At Gwen's side was Grant Jordan, his clothes white with trail dust, his face angry. She was relieved to see him.

Jordan stepped from the boardwalk and stood over Clum, who was slightly stunned. Clum shook his head to clear it and looked up at Jordan, who said softly, "Didn't mean to take you by surprise, pardner. Stand up and see one comin'."

Gwen didn't think Clum would try anything even though he was broader and heavier than Jordan. But she was wrong: Clum was angry, and he was game. He lurched to his feet and yanked off his suit jacket and waistcoat. A crowd was quickly gathering as the freighter, with madness in his eye, abruptly lunged at Jordan.

The attack surprised the hunter, and he was off balance when Clum bowled into him, but he absorbed the charge, took Clum by the shoulders, and jerked him over a hitching rail, narrowly missing a horse trough full of water. Someone in the milling crowd near the trough squealed, "Two to one Jess Clum takes a bath afore this is done!" "You're on for five!" another shouted back.

Clum was winded, but he sprang to his feet, close to Gwen. He looked like a wild animal, she thought, and her heart skipped. Clum began to circle Jordan, clearly wanting to wrestle and use his superior strength and weight. Jordan was set up with his left fist leading, a boxing stance. Clum made his move, lunging forward again, but Jordan stepped into it this time, sticking a straight left very hard into Clum's face—a wicked whack that got a roar from the crowd—following quickly with a right, another left, and then a jarring right-hand uppercut that staggered Clum backward into the arms of the man who had bet on him getting a ducking. His face bleeding badly, Clum collapsed upon the fellow, unconscious. Looking around before giving a shrug of his shoulders, the man who had caught Clum gave a little push, and the freighter fell headfirst into the horse trough. "Pay me!" he said to his friend, who did.

Men shouted their admiration to Jordan, who was staring down at Clum and rubbing his cut knuckles. That last hit was hard enough to keep the man out for some time. He stepped to the trough and dragged Clum out of the water, then laid him facedown on the boardwalk at Gwen's feet. Jordan looked up at her, and her eyes were bright. With a wry smile, he said, "That Delmonico's feed would suit me just now."

A little while later, Meeker joined them at the Chicago House, with lazy Misty tagging along, and they had lunch. As they sat at a red and white checked luncheon table in the sunny restaurant, Jordan told them he intended staying in the hotel for the night, then departing after they hired men to

escort Gwen. The conversation died soon after that. Gwen
was thinking she might never see Jordan again, and he was
thinking the same about her. Meeker chose not to speak. He
had seen much, this old man, and he saw what was between
these two young people—more than either of them saw. He
knew, however, that Jordan was not a man to change his
mind easily and settle down for the winter at the Quinn mine.
But if Jordan went on this mission with Gwen, Meeker
figured that was exactly what would happen, and he knew
that thought was in the back of Jordan's mind, too. Meeker
could see this young fellow was reluctant to stop roaming, to
make a life that was more than buffalo hunting, Indian lodges,
mining camps, and one-night women.

If Jordan could have read Meeker's thoughts, he would
have laughed at them, though he would not have disagreed.
But any growing feelings he had for Gwen were still not
obvious to Jordan. As far as she was concerned, he thought
only of getting her off to a good start. But first, he said, he
intended to visit the Crows who had arrived. He got up to go,
and Gwen asked carefully, "Grant . . . what about my . . .
cousins?"

Jordan touched her hand, resting on the table, and said,
"They're taken care of. Let them rest where they are."

They held each other's eyes for a moment; then she nodded
and wiped away a tear. Jordan left, saying he would see them
after he came back from the Indians that afternoon.

As Jordan rode the Appaloosa out Cover Street past the
army camp, he saw the entire company of forty soldiers busy
with gear and horses, as though they were going somewhere.
He spotted Billy Buchanan walking along and called to him.
Buchanan looked up, still dirty and dusty from the patrol
recently completed, and shouted, "Looks like we're going to
the Crows." Then he jerked his thumb in the direction of a

party of men under the command of Lieutenant Wilkinson. They were hauling a tarpaulin from the Gatling gun. Jordan didn't like it. He watched as the lieutenant stood behind the gun, which was shaped like a field cannon, with large wheels, but had ten barrels that revolved when fired and operated by a hand crank. It was rated at four hundred rounds a minute.

Wilkinson tested the crank and spun the firing tubes on their chassis. Then he slapped the weapon top and made a joke with the soldiers, who laughed and dragged the gun to a caisson, as yet not hitched to a team of horses.

Jordan spurred the horse and galloped down the road, past the coolies in the Ruby Creek gully and over a rise that kept the Indian camp out of sight from the town. He grew angry and worried as he rode. He did not know what he would do when he found the Crows or what to tell them. But he had to go to them.

When he crested the rise, he reined in and stared down at the small camp. It was worse than he had thought. There were few women and no children in sight, mostly males. At least if the Crows had come with their families, Rutledge might have been restrained from taking any rash action. Jordan pushed his horse ahead, and the Indians turned to watch him come. There were fewer than sixty of them, mostly old men and boys, it seemed, although there were a few bucks among them who had not gone hunting with the other young men.

As Jordan neared the clutter of fifteen tepees still being erected or already up, he recognized this band. These were the followers of Chief Hoko-lana, a people Jordan had wintered with four years before and who had taken him in time and again since then. The Crows, who provided many scouts for the army, were notably peaceful Indians when it came to contact with whites, and Hoko-lana's folk were among the friendliest of the lot.

Dogs barked, boys shouted welcome to him, and a young brave in a bright-red shirt grabbed the bridle of Jordan's horse. This was Kintara, son of the chief, a slender, wiry fellow of nineteen, dark-eyed and handsome, with waist-length black hair in the Crow warrior fashion. Jordan sprang from the horse, and Kintara gave the bridle to another, throwing his arms around Jordan, happy to see him.

"Have you not gone to the buffalo hunting?" Kintara asked in the Crow tongue. "My unmarried sister did not come here with us but went north with my uncle because he was going to the buffalo, and she thought she would share your lodge up there for the winter!"

Jordan grinned. "Your little sister needs a husband, not a man who is only passing through as I will always be. And you, Kintara, why do you not hunt? Why are you here for the government goods?"

Kintara's bright happiness at seeing Jordan faded quickly. He shook his head, and his eyes clouded over. "It has been bad with us, Jordan. Sickness, fever came among us in the warm months, and many have died. We need the government treaty goods, and we were told by the Indian agent to come here because a journey to the Yellowstone agency would be too hard for those who are still weak. I came here because I want to watch over the talks, and I want to see that my people are not cheated as they have been in the past. We need much, Jordan, and we must have it before this winter or we go under. . . ."

So much hardship, and now they had Rutledge, too, Jordan thought bleakly. He went with Kintara to the lodge of Chief Hoko-lana, ducking under the deerskin flap and entering the cozy tepee, where a small fire already burned, though the lodge had not been up an hour. Hoko-lana, a wrinkled but sturdy old warrior, sat proud and erect, wearing a black cloak. The chief was delighted to see Jordan, and they smoked the pipe with glad hearts before speaking, as Indian courtesy required. Jordan waited with his bad news, but he sensed he could not wait long. The hair on the back of his neck prickled as he thought of the soldiers and the Gatling gun.

After he had been in the dim lodge for ten minutes, the time was right, and he apologized for bringing troublesome news. He told of the hostilities to the south, and Hoko-lana and Kintara listened glumly as Jordan said Captain Rutledge was on his way, adding that they should be wary in dealing with him. When Jordan finished, the Indians sat in thought a moment. Then Hoko-lana said he would call in his subchiefs to discuss this matter. He added that he was sure no Crows were causing the trouble, but he had no idea what tribe was guilty.

Before Jordan could say there was little time to prepare for the parley with Rutledge, a shout of excitement swept through the Indian camp, voices crying that bluecoats were coming. Hoko-lana put on an eagle-feather headdress and went outside, followed by Jordan and Kintara.

Jordan saw the soldiers up on the crest of the ridge overlooking the camp. The men were in battle line of two ranks. The Gatling and its caisson were off to the right as he looked at the unit, and in the center was the troop flag and an American flag. At the fore was Rutledge, followed by Lieutenant Wilkinson. Jordan thought he saw a civilian with the captain, and he took his binoculars from his horse's saddle and looked. It was Jess Clum. How did he fit into this?

The Indians were excited, many showing anger and fear, others fetching weapons, expecting the worst. With the defeat of Custer the previous year and the campaign against the Nez Percé going on at that moment, these Crows were worried about overeager cavalry commanders. Now Hoko-lana's men and boys were arming themselves, some carrying good Winchesters and pistols but most with dilapidated trade guns, old single-shot hunting rifles, and even a few bows in the hands of the youngest boys. This was what Jordan was afraid of.

He called to the chief and Kintara, "Keep your people calm," he said, looking out at the cavalry moving slowly down the slope toward the Indians. "Don't give the soldiers cause to start anything!"

The Indian leaders understood, and word passed quickly through the motley crowd, although there were a few older bucks who did not like what they saw. One or two shouted that they should fetch the pony herd into camp and hold the horses ready to fight. Hoko-lana looked at Jordan, who saw the horses grazing on bunchgrass a hundred yards east of the camp. The soldiers were coming from the south, moving at an angle across the front of the camp, as though intending to cut the Indians off from their mounts. Jordan looked back at Hoko-lana and shook his head sharply. Any dash for the ponies might set off Rutledge, who was no doubt well bolstered with liquor by now. Hoko-lana ordered his men to be calm, and the more solid ones moved behind their chief as he stepped forward to meet the approaching soldiers.

Jordan moved out of sight behind a tepee and waited. The soldiers rode down to about thirty yards from where Hoko-lana and Kintara stood with half a dozen other braves beside them. Slowly, deliberately, the cavalry fanned out in a half circle around the camp, between the Indians and their ponies. All this time, Rutledge sat his horse, scowling down at the Crow chief, not saying a word. His eyes were stern, like an angry father's. Hoko-lana raised his hand in the sign of peace, but Rutledge made no reply.

The atmosphere was tense, explosive. Hoko-lana did not give an inch, but raised his head and looked Rutledge in the eye, saying, "The soldier chief comes with his young men armed, with the wheel gun that speaks many times . . . does he come in friendship or as an enemy?"

Then Jordan realized why Clum was there, for the freighter had ridden forward to Captain Rutledge's side and was translating Hoko-lana's words. Even from where Jordan stood, another twenty yards away, he could see the black-and-blue bruise on Clum's forehead, where he had been hit in their fight. Another reddish welt showed on Clum's left cheekbone, and his face was puffy. The translation was correct, but Jordan thought he would listen a moment longer before showing himself. That way he might learn more about this man Clum.

Rutledge's reply was harsh and inflammatory, nearly insulting, as he told Hoko-lana that the Crows had not kept faith with the government, accusing the Crows of letting their young men prey on helpless wagoneers and ending with the blunt question "What do you think the Great Father in Washington will do to the Crows when he hears of their bad hearts?" Again, Clum's translation was accurate.

Hoko-lana thought a moment, then said slowly, "It is not our custom to speak of such profound matters under the hot eye of the sun. If the soldier chief will join us in our tepee, we shall smoke in friendship, and then the words of the Crows shall be spoken, not from a bad heart but from a heart that is true."

Clum translated, saying to Rutledge, "The old man says what you're saying is a lie, and he wants to show you how friendly the Crows really are by giving you a smoke of tobacco in his lodge."

Rutledge looked even more grim as he blustered, "There will be no counsel, no tobacco, and no government goods until I am promised immediately that his people will give up their weapons and depart from here in peace!"

Clum said to the chief, "To prove that your hearts are true and to spread the balm of trust on our own hearts, which are sore from the deaths of our people, you must surrender your guns immediately to the soldier chief. Then you will receive the governmemt supplies, and you may depart in peace, without your teeth and claws.''

The Crows stirred angrily, some of them gripping weapons to their chests as Clum translated. Hoko-lana stood at his full height and said again, ''It is not the custom of the Crows to speak of such matters under the hot eye of the sun, soldier chief. If you wish to speak with me, then come to my lodge.''

With that, Hoko-lana whirled, his cloak flowing, feathers flitting in the wind, and strode back to his tepee. Kintara moved with him, casting a wary glance over his shoulder at the soldiers as he went.

''What's he doing?'' Rutledge demanded of Clum.

Clum replied, ''Says you have no right to speak to a Crow chief that way, Captain. He wants you to apologize before he'll treat with you!''

''What?'' Rutledge was bursting with indignation. He waved to the Gatling gun crew, and Lieutenant Wilkinson obediently directed his men in unlimbering it from the caisson. The Indians chattered nervously and drew back. Hoko-lana was almost at the entrance of his lodge when Jordan stepped into the crowd of Indians and walked toward Rutledge, who was clearly incensed to see him among the Crows. Clum was also startled, jerking his head when he saw Jordan.

''What the hell do you want here?'' Rutledge stood up in the stirrups as he challenged Jordan. The Gatling gun was being brought to bear on the Indians, who were crowded in the middle of the half-erected camp. Hoko-lana and Kintara had stopped and turned to watch Jordan confront the soldiers.

''This man's lying to you,'' Jordan said to Rutledge, indicating Clum with a wave of the hand. ''The Crows haven't insulted you, but they don't like the army pointing guns at them and demanding to parley.''

"Whatever they like or don't like is of no concern to me, sir!" Rutledge said, making a fist at Jordan. "They'll obey military directives or face the consequences. Now you tell them to give up their guns, and then we'll talk in that old buzzard's lodge or out of it, I don't care! But I want those guns in military hands so they won't be used to murder innocent people! Understand? Tell your friends that!"

Jordan stared at Rutledge, then slowly turned to Hoko-lana, who was watching, eyes dark and angry. Jordan told the chief what Rutledge had said, and Hoko-lana came back to his side, looking up at Rutledge.

"I will talk first," Hoko-lana said slowly. "I will talk with the soldier chief out here, but I will give up no weapons. We have come for what our treaty gives us, and we are guilty of no crime, nor of breaking our treaty. I will talk with the soldier chief, and we will not smoke the pipe. But no guns will we surrender."

Jordan translated, and Rutledged looked to Clum, who nodded to concur with the translation. Exasperated, Rutledge gritted his teeth, then said, "We'll talk first. All right. But only on the condition that you, sir, keep clear of this!"

He dismounted, as did Clum. The Gatling gun was not far away, its threat hanging over the parley as an ominous warning to the Crows. As the talks began, Jordan moved off on his own, edging toward the Gatling. The Indian leaders sat on the ground before Rutledge and Clum, who had been brought folding chairs by the soldiers. The other Indians huddled a little way back among the tepees, still holding their precious weapons. Jordan knew that for an Indian to give up his gun was to be humiliated, and losing a gun would make hunting for food nearly impossible. Even though the government provided some supplies, the Crows needed to hunt to survive. Why, Jordan wondered, was Rutledge willing to push this thing so hard with the Crows? Did he really want a fight here? If one came, the Crows had no chance against the Gatling, and every man there knew it.

And what about Clum? That question also troubled Jordan. What did Clum have to do with this, and why did he seem so fired up to see the army and the Crows go at it? As Jordan stepped close to the Gatling, where three soldiers and Lieutenant Wilkinson were standing, he saw Billy Buchanan mounted a few feet away. Buchanan looked unhappy, as did many of the soldiers and a few Pawnee army scouts watching this confrontation unfold. But not Lieutenant Wilkinson. As he stood at the Gatling, Wilkinson was the picture of discipline, tight-lipped and humorless, staring at Rutledge as though eager for the command that would permit him to open up with the deadly rapid-fire gun.

As Jordan stepped close, Wilkinson broke his stiff bearing and waved a hand, motioning him to stay out of the firing line. Jordan spat, folded his arms, and smiled blankly. He moved a little out of the way, but not enough for Wilkinson, who waved even harder at him.

Jordan's mind was racing. He knew Clum would likely be translating Hoko-lana's words in a way that would enrage Rutledge. Clum was bent on causing trouble—that was sure—and Jordan was not certain he could do anything to stop it. But if trouble did break out, then he wanted to be where he could do the Crows the most good. It meant obstructing the army. It probably meant he would go to jail . . . if he lived through it. Grant Jordan was a man without commitments, and that made him ready to accept whatever might come if he had to fight the federal army. Already, he had passed the point where discretion should have told him to stop.

He let Wilkinson have his way and stepped back a little more from the gun. Jordan was ready now, his whole being taut for what he would do if a fight began. He only hoped he would not have to kill anyone.

As he listened to the men parleying about sixty feet away, he sized up the scene. The Indian males slightly outnumbered the soldiers but were poorly armed. Against the Gatling gun, they were helpless. Also, the soldiers had cut off the Indians from their horses, so if something started, the Crows would be fighting on foot, the soldiers mounted. He saw Kintara, his face drawn and showing barely contained aggression. The young warrior was standing back from where Hoko-lana and another old chief were seated talking with Rutledge and Clum. Near Kintara, who carried a new Winchester rifle, were a dozen of the older boys and a few braves. All were silent, all extremely sullen, with hate in their eyes. The handful of women who had come with the party were at the rear of the men, and Jordan noticed several had picked up knives; one even had a pistol in her hand.

Jordan noticed two or three young bucks drifting in the direction of the horses. Apparently, neither Kintara nor Hoko-lana saw the young men making their way out of the encampment, strolling casually toward the ponies. But some soldiers saw them and moved their horses over so the braves could not easily pass. This all took place seventy or eighty yards from where Jordan stood, and he had the tepees partly in the way, so it was difficult to see what was happening over there.

By now, the talk between Rutledge and Hoko-lana had become animated. The disagreement had reached a head, Jordan thought. He saw Rutledge pound his fist into the palm of his hand, then wave a warning finger in the air. As though that were a signal, Lieutenant Wilkinson moved with his crew to the firing position at the Gatling. What this meant, Jordan was not sure, but he didn't like it. Perhaps this was simply all a ploy to frighten the Indians, who did not miss seeing the crew take its stations around the gun. A few soldiers grew restless in the saddle. They had not failed to recognize the temper of the Indians, and every man in the semicircular line was ready for whatever might come. The Crow women shifted from foot to foot, those who were unarmed locking fingers and unlocking them, a few holding hands, and all looking to their men for a sign.

But their men were too distracted to communicate with them. As though acting with mutual understanding, the men had formed a defensive ring around the women at the center of the camp, feeble weapons bristling in their hands.

Jordan was about to talk to Rutledge when suddenly, across the camp, there was a flurry of activity and a shout from a soldier. A cavalryman was riding at a brave on foot, forcing him away from the pony herd, which spooked and began to mill. The young Indian stood still as the rider bore down on him, the horseman reining in at the last minute before his mount would have ridden the Crow down. It was a standoff between the trooper and the brave. All eyes turned to the drama as the trooper motioned with his head for the Indian to get back with his people. The Crow did not move. Other Indians began to approach, and Kintara hurried through the camp to see what he could do.

"Get out of the way, Jordan, damn you!"

That was Wilkinson from behind the Gatling. Jordan had again worked himself into the line of fire. He did not turn around to answer Wilkinson. Another trooper spurred his horse to join the first soldier facing down the brave who would not back off. Now there were four or five young braves and two or three boys anxious to show their courage, and the situation near the horses was in need of cool heads on both sides. The two troopers were whirling their mounts and bumping the armed braves with the shoulders of their horses.

Jordan was glad Kintara was going to calm down his people. He wished Rutledge would do the same.

From behind, someone shoved him hard, sending him off

balance so that he barely kept his feet. He spun to see Wilkinson shaking a finger at him. "And keep out of the way, you! Do it again and you'll be locked—"

A woman screamed. Jordan looked to the trouble near the Indian ponies and saw a soldier's horse rear. A Crow was lying on the ground. Other Crows were shouting and moving quickly toward the two troopers. The cavalryman fought to control his rearing horse. Rutledge looked up and blared out an order that was hard to hear over the din of the Indians. A few soldiers were calling to their friends, and four more troopers galloped toward the disturbance. Another Indian went down, and Jordan saw a soldier's saber flash in the sunlight. The tumult grew, and he heard a war whoop, then another, then a shout from Rutledge again, and Wilkinson ran back behind the gun.

Jordan's mind kept echoing, over and over, *No! Don't let this happen! No!*

The soldiers coming to their comrades' assistance bowled over some braves and nearly ran down the women as they pounded through the Indian camp. One trooper hooked a hand on uncovered tepee poles and yanked. Down came the poles, falling into a fire. Squaws screeched and wailed, horses whinnied, Rutledge shrieked for order, and then came the shot. Who fired it was unclear, but that did not matter. Clum ran away from where he sat opposite Hoko-lana, seeking the shelter of the line of troopers, and Rutledge jerked his sword from its scabbard, backing off as he did so.

Wilkinson was at the Gatling, waiting for an order. Hoko-lana was looking at the confused scene of fighting across the camp, and then came another shot, and another. A trooper on the other side of the camp was dragged from his horse.

"Move or I'll kill you if I have to!" Wilkinson blared at Jordan, who stood facing him, his chest inches from the Gatling barrel. Jordan knew that it would be more difficult to explain away the killing of a white man than it would the massacre of an Indian camp.

"Jordan!" That was Buchanan, who rode toward him, then looked at Wilkinson, but reined in and said no more.

Now Hoko-lana had his hands out as though imploring Rutledge to try to stabilize the situation. But Hoko-lana was alone. The other elders were drawing back among the anxious braves, who were clustered together like a herd of buffalo facing wolves.

Wilkinson shouted and charged around the gun at Jordan, who flattened him with one well-placed punch to the head. Another soldier leaped at Jordan, and he dropped the man before the fellow could swing. Then another trooper and another came at him, and all the while, the tumult in the camp was rising. Jordan took a couple of hard knocks, but he held his ground, fighting back the cavalrymen, hearing Rutledge shout, "Stop that man! Arrest that man!"

Three soldiers lay at Jordan's feet, and another grabbed him from behind. Jordan flipped the man over his head and booted him in the face when he tried to get up. Wilkinson was scrambling away. Jordan stood over the four troopers and saw Rutledge coming at him, shouting, "Stop!"

Now three, four, five guns went off. A few soldiers began to draw their pistols. Jordan saw Hoko-lana turn to the soldiers again, raising his hands to prevent firing. Rutledge was shaking his saber at Jordan. Wilkinson was behind the gun, madly screaming, "What shall I do, sir, what shall I do?" Jordan was still in the Gatling's line of fire. It was now or never. His Rebel heritage rose to the crest once again, and he knew how he must finish this fight—on the side of the Crows, even to the end. He whipped out his revolver and was turning to wound Wilkinson when a massive weight came down on his shoulders, buckling his legs and driving him hard to the ground. A powerful hand ripped his pistol away, and as he fought to break free, he heard wild shooting, screaming, and horses neighing in terror, and over it all rose William Rutledge's frantic voice. "Fire! Open fire, Wilkinson! Kill them all!"

Jordan shouted and heaved up with all his might, tossing off the man who had him down. In that same instant, a savage burst of gunfire roared near his head. The Gatling! He scrambled up and charged Wilkinson, just barely able to see for the dirt and sweat in his eyes. Wilkinson yelped and jumped back as Jordan came at him. But before he got to Wilkinson, that same huge weight crushed Jordan again, and he was yanked away and driven with stunning impact into the dusty earth. The last thing he knew was the voice of Billy Buchanan shouting, as though from far away, "Don't shoot! I got 'im! Don't shoot 'im, sir!"

Chapter 7

A throbbing pain seemed to have separated Grant Jordan's head from his shoulders. He could almost hear the ache pound through his skull, like a mill wheel grinding. Voices were there, too, somewhere, but he could not make out who they were or what they were talking about. He felt at his head. Where was he? On his back? Above was the blue sky, fuzzy, coming and going. There was a shadow there . . . a face. A voice. Buchanan. Then another voice. He was on his back, all right. *What am I doing on my back?*

And then it began to take form in his mind—the army, Crows, Hoko-lana . . . the Gatling! He groaned against the pain and gritted his teeth. Someone was holding him down. Buchanan's voice again . . . "He's out for a while, Cap'n . . . let me take him in . . . he won't be no more trouble, sir." Jordan tried to get up, but everything was out of focus, off balance. Oh, how his head pounded!

Another voice, harsh and cutting: ". . . better not give us any more trouble! I've got a mind to leave him with the Indians, the Rebel bastard!"

Still another voice, smooth and confident: "Yes, sir, Captain Rutledge, he's just like them—a renegade. Didn't learn his lesson when he got his ass kicked as a Rebel, so now he's an Indian-loving renegade. . . ."

"You got no cause to talk like that—" Billy's voice was hot and boiling over.

Tell him, Billy! If only I could get up!

"That's enough, Sergeant!" Jordan now recognized Rutledge speaking. "We'll detail a guard to get this renegade back to camp, and we'll hold a military trial tomorrow. No use letting the likes of him run loose! He's already attacked Mr. Clum here, and it's time he got what's coming to him! On your way, Sergeant!"

"But, sir—"

"Damn it, man! Do you want to share the jailhouse with him? I don't forget your own Confederate origins, either, you know!"

Jordan's eyes were clearing now. He saw Billy rise and walk away. Rutledge was motioning for some men to come and pick Jordan up, and he found Clum standing over him, his handsome face smug and contented as he stared down.

"Looks like you picked the wrong time and place to fight the army again, Johnny Reb," Clum said. "You Rebs don't ever learn, do you—?"

That was Clum's last smile for a while because Jordan summoned all his strength and kicked wickedly, catching Clum between the legs and knocking a howl of agony from him. Then two soldiers had Jordan back on the ground, pinning his shoulders. Clum, enraged, tried to get at him, a rifle in his hands, the butt raised to smash Jordan's face. But a blur of blue swept in between, and Clum was knocked away. Again, Jordan heard Billy Buchanan roar, "No call for that!"

"Sergeant Buchanan!" Rutledge was there again. "Let Mr. Clum up! You hear! Get off him!"

"Yes, sir, Cap'n. Jus' didn't want Mr. Clum to get another beatin' from that Johnny Reb there. You know how Johnny Rebs can be when they hold a grudge agin the likes o' Mr. Clum—"

Rutledge swore and again ordered Buchanan away. It was obvious that Rutledge commanded little respect from his troops, for one of the cavalrymen holding Jordan down whispered, "We'll keep that bastard off you, friend. Just don't give him the boot again."

Jordan looked up at the man, a middle-aged, brown-toothed veteran, who winked. Then Jordan was being helped to his feet while Rutledge squawked at his men, ordering the troops to return to camp. Though his head still hurt from being slammed when taken down earlier, Jordan could see well enough now, and when he got up and looked at what had once been the Indian camp, his heart skipped.

There was nothing he could say when he saw thirty bodies littering the ground, sprawled in all sorts of awkward positions, like bundles of rags. At least half the Crows had been shot down. A few were still moving, and what appeared to be a military medical crew was ministering to them. Jordan swayed, almost fainting from the shock, but the troopers holding him lifted his arms over their shoulders, the one with the stained teeth saying softly, "Weren't our doin', pard. Was that Gatlin' what cut 'em down. Most o' the boys didn't even draw pistols. That dirty little Wilkinson an' his Gatlin' cut your Injun friends down . . . understand that."

Jordan's fury gave him strength again. Wilkinson and Rutledge were only a few feet away. Jordan took deep breaths and concentrated on their backs. When he had the power, he would go for them, and he would kill one before—

"Easy!" the trooper said, and gripped his wrist as it dangled over the man's shoulder. "We ain't lettin' you get loose, boy, so don't get no fool ideas. Easy now."

Jordan felt the two soldiers tighten their holds on his wrists and put their arms firmly around his waist. He was too weak to get away from them, and he knew it. The trooper was speaking again. ". . . this'll come to a hearin', pard, an' there's enough of us will back you up. . . . You kin thank Billy Buchanan fer savin' your life. If he hadn't tooken you down, the cap'n would've plugged you . . . would've done it even with you down if Billy hadn't laid on you, coverin' you up till the killin' was done. . . ." Jordan listened, his head spinning as a spell of dizziness overcame him, and he began to break into a sweat. The soldiers were walking him away, and all the while, the trooper was telling what happened. Apparently, a number of Indians—mostly the older bucks—had escaped. They had reached their horses, and the soldiers did little to stop them after the first disturbance. When the troopers saw the Gatling go into action, most wanted the Crows to escape, not favoring a slaughter, and they let them go, making only a show of trying to oppose the braves.

Jordan soon found himself lying on his back on some sort of wagon. He felt the rig jerk as a driver slapped the reins on the team, and the conveyance began to move away. Jordan propped himself up and asked the trooper, who sat nearby, "What about their chief? What—"

The trooper shook his head slowly. "The old feller's done for. Got the Gatlin' full front. Not much left even to bury. Sorry, pard." Jordan sank back, his mind sad and lost, wandering with the images of friends among the people of Hoko-lana. He asked about Kintara, and the trooper listened to a description of the chief's son before saying, "He's one that got away. Young buck, he was? Red shirt and white leggin's? Yep, saw him skedaddle with a few o' his boys. Coulda plugged 'im myself easy enough, but he's gone.''

Jordan lay, half sitting up, while the rig bumped and lurched back toward Virginia City. The ringing in his head had stopped, and he noticed a few civilians riding out on horses and mules to see what had happened. The firing had likely stirred up the whole town, and sightseers would be coming in droves now that the lead had stopped flying.

Then Jordan wondered just what he was being carried in, and he craned his neck to look at the rig. His heart sank, and his head throbbed even harder when he saw he was on the caisson pulling the murderous Gatling gun.

"Grant! Grant!"

Jordan looked up from where he lay across the caisson and saw Gwen running alongside, her face anxious and afraid. They were coming into the army camp on Cover Street.

"I heard what happened!" she called, trotting all the while. "It's a terrible thing! Are you all right?"

The caisson lurched to a stop, and Jordan was helped out by his guard. Gwen came to him, her hands touching the lump on the side of his head, her eyes searching his. He took her hand from the bruise and said, "Looks like I'll have some business with the army, Gwen. See Billy for the help you need."

The guard urged him ahead toward the crowd of tents, saying Jordan would have to be locked in a clapboard storehouse for now. Tomorrow he would be transferred to the town jail after the official forms were filled out by the army. But the soldier did not rush the couple as Gwen asked Jordan if there was anything she could do. Amos had heard about the Indian killing, and he had told her how Jordan had interfered with the soldiers.

"No, girl, there's nothin' you can do," he said, but wanted

to ease her troubled heart. "I'll be glad to know you got through to your pa. Maybe I'll be passin' through here again, and I'll stop by and see that gold you're so sure is up there."

Then the guards led him away to a storage shed forty yards from the army tents. Anger mingled with fright inside Gwen as she stared at Jordan's back while he walked to the shed. She watched the guards open the door, lead Jordan inside, and then close the door again and padlock it.

Something had to be done! Maybe she could pay for a good lawyer to defend him—but she had so little time to spare here in Virginia City. She had to find a lawyer fast; then she had to see Buchanan to hire the men needed as her escort. Her whole being was torn between staying and helping Jordan or hurrying back to the mine. Gwen left the army camp, walking fast back to the Chicago House along Cover Street when a voice called to her. She turned to see Billy Buchanan, who dismounted and touched his hat, his face downcast and worried.

"He's gone an' done it now, miss. He's in real trouble."

"I know," Gwen nodded, and fought back a trembling inside her. "I'm going to hire a lawyer . . . whatever I can do."

Buchanan shook his head. "Lawyer won't do much good, I'd say. Rutledge can put Jordan away in the can for a good long time. Says he's a renegade, an' he'll try to blame Jordan for stirrin' up them redskins. I don't like to think what the army could do. . . . It don't look good for the boy, no, not at all."

They spoke a few more minutes, and Gwen learned that some of the soldiers might testify in Jordan's favor if they were called to a witness stand, but if the Crows were found to have started the trouble, there was really very little the soldiers could say that would change matters much. The fact was that Jordan had interfered with the Gatling gun crew, and he fought with Wilkinson and other soldiers. That made him guilty of obstructing military operations. The turning point of Jordan's defense lay in whether it could be proved beyond doubt that the Crows were friendly and that Captain Rutledge had recklessly instigated the fight. Proving that, said Buchanan, was not going to be easy, particularly in light of past hostilities, such as the ambush of Gwen's stagecoach. It was obvious—particularly from Jordan's own earlier comment about the culprits in that stagecoach attack resembling Crows—that Hoko-lana's people could be suspected as renegades. With the current public fear of a mass Indian uprising—the Nez Percé campaign and the defeat of Custer being ample testimony to the hostile state of mind of many tribes—the general feeling on the part of the military might be to support Rutledge and condemn Jordan.

"Condemn him . . . to what?" Gwen asked the sergeant.

"Whites who fight for the Injuns can be executed," he said. "The gallows . . ." His voice choked up.

Neither spoke as they stood in the street with crowds of people swirling past them, all on their way to or from the destroyed Indian camp. Some were laughing and joking about the fight, glad the Indians had been punished; others were angry that a few had escaped. Gwen thought of what Buchanan had said: Jordan might be hanged by the army. She looked at Buchanan. "We can't let them do that, Billy. We can't."

Buchanan rubbed his grizzled chin a moment and stood deep in thought. He took off his hat and scratched his head. Then he put it back and gave a deep sigh. "You know, girl, I never have felt quite right about wearin' Yankee blue; no, not in all these years." He rubbed the sergeant's chevrons on his bicep, then slapped them. "And I suppose these stripes are worth Grant Jordan's life."

Gwen wondered what exactly he was getting at, but in the

back of her mind, she had the idea. Buchanan looked around quickly and saw there were no soldiers nearby; then, taking her arm and leading her away, he said, "Why don't we have a little parley with your friend Amos Meeker, and if you really want to help Jordan, then listen . . ."

It was night, and Jordan lay on bags of seed corn that were piled on each other until they half filled the little shed. The building belonged to a farmer who had rented the land to the army for the temporary camp. It was decrepit, but solid enough to keep him prisoner. He had tried the door already, crashing against it a few times in pure meanness, venting his frustration and anger until the guard outside told him to stop before Lieutenant Wilkinson heard it and got it in his mind to make more trouble for Jordan.

There were no illusions in Grant Jordan's mind. From the first, when he fought with the soldiers at the Gatling, he knew the consequences. He knew a military trial would go hard on him, but he did not regret what he had done. Rather, he wished he had done more. He wished he had taken over that gun and turned it on Rutledge and Clum. Clum! That snake had caused much of this trouble! Why? The man had a freight line to run, and his wagons would be in constant danger as long as there were hostile Indians on the loose. Surely Clum did not think that shooting up Hoko-lana's people would stop the trouble that had been going on. Clum might just be an Indian hater who liked to see them bleed. But, no, he was too businesslike, too shrewd in manipulating Rutledge to have contrived the massacre just for the sake of killing. There had to be another reason that Clum wanted trouble with the Crows, but Jordan had not the faintest notion.

"Hey, you cotton picker, you still in there?" That was Buchanan's voice at the door, and Jordan heard him knock faintly.

"No," Jordan replied. "I'm dinin' out tonight with Rutledge. Hey, Billy, when do they serve dinner in this hotel? I haven't eaten since I checked in."

"What's that you say?" Buchanan was fumbling with the chain lock. "You're sick?"

"I'm not sick, just hungry. And bring me some water—"

"Sick, you say? Like to die?"

The door swung creaking open, and a little light from the oil lamps hanging on poles in the camp filtered into the dark shed. Buchanan's massive silhouette blocked the doorway.

"Can't you understand American, boy?" Jordan asked, his bones stiff and sore, his head still painful as he made to rise from his bed of seed bags. "I'm hungry, not sick—"

"Well bless my Georgia soul, you cotton picker, you do look sick . . . sick to death, boy. Come here; let me help you up." Buchanan took Jordan by the arm and lifted him. Jordan tried to protest that he was all right except for his sore head and empty stomach, but Buchanan kept babbling about sickness.

"Got to get you to the medical officer right away, boy. Just lucky I happened to come by and relieve the trooper on duty. I convinced him he had to take a leak, an' he did have to after he guzzled some o' that Valley Tan he found in my back pocket. Varmint took the bottle to the latrine with him, too, greedy cuss. Yep, that guard never woulda thought to look in on his prisoner, an' you woulda likely been shriveled up an' dead by mornin', an' that ain't sportin', no, not when the United States Army aims to kill you official-like. . . ."

All this time, Jordan was being led outside, until he realized what was happening and he stopped, interrupting Buchanan. "Billy, you're playin' with fire. They'll hang you instead—"

"Shut up, boy. I declare you Johnny Rebs talk too much an' think too much. Why I was jest this afternoon sayin' to that little Miss Quinn what runners-off-at-the-mouth Rebels can be, an' she agreed with me. She said you talk more than most, an' if you don't believe me, then jest ask her yourself. She's right over there on Cover Street, her an' that old-timer, takin' in the night air, I reckon. An' by the way, they're walkin' your horses in case you can't find the time while you're restin' up in this shed, specially bein' as you're sick an' all. Easy now, don't go so fast, you'll faint, boy. . . ."

Buchanan was moving slowly toward the clump of army tents, among which was the medical officer's quarters. Jordan knew what Buchanan was doing, but he presumed his friend had a plan, and he wanted to let it unravel before he made a try to escape.

Now Buchanan was saying, "Hell, Jordan, you're gettin' old, you are. You went down easier'n my ma's peach pie this afternoon. I took you down like a rag doll! Shucks! I was a little embarrassed to treat you so rough, but when I first knew you up on the Yellowstone, you was a tough hoss, an' it took a good lick to put you out. But I didn't even work up a sweat today. I thought you'd get a lick or two in when I went for you, but no . . . why I reckon you tried, but missed. . . ."

In the dimness of the slumbering army camp, Buchanan had stopped, facing Jordan, sticking his jaw out. "Why I thought you mighta caught me one good one jest to make things interestin'. You know, right here on my chin, on the good side, where one lucky hit sometimes makes me see stars. Shucks! The boys been makin' jokes all day 'bout how rough I was with you, an' I'll have to live it down or whup 'em all again. Why I reckon you need to practice some, Jordan. You know, do a little sparrin' with somebody as can't hit back. That way you won't get hurt an' you'll learn somethin' about—"

Jordan's fist slammed Buchanan's upthrust jaw, and the sergeant stumbled backward and fell heavily. Jordan went quickly to his side, knelt over him, and saw he was unconscious. Then he looked about the camp. Nothing was stirring but the wind billowing canvas tents. He looked back at his friend, sorry to have punched him that way but realizing that he had to make the escape look real or Buchanan would be accused of helping him.

Jordan got to his feet and looked toward Cover Street, where Billy said Gwen and Meeker were waiting with the horses. He glanced down at Buchanan briefly and said, "Sorry, Billy. I didn't want to do that."

Buchanan's head came up. "Sorry? I was right, old hoss. You can't hit like you used to! Now git! They're waitin', an' the guard'll be back right quick!"

Jordan touched his friend's hand and then, in a crouch, hurried through the outskirts of the camp, making for darkened, deserted Cover Street. In a few moments, he found Gwen and Meeker standing in the deeper darkness of a barn with his own animals as well as new mounts of their own and another packhorse. Gwen ran to him and put her head against his chest, holding him close.

"I'm all right!" he said. "Just give me my horses and I'll be on my way!"

"Be careful, Grant," she replied, and he saw her eyes gleaming in the faint light.

"You, too. Where you going?"

Meeker's sharp whisper came to them. "Let's get out of town, fast. You can say good-byes up in the hills! Come on!"

They walked the horses a little way to the end of Cover Street, then mounted and rode hard along the road through the gulch. After three hundred yards, they turned off, with Meeker leading the way, and went up a narrow trail into the hills above the town, which slumbered far below in the darkness, showing a few points of light here and there.

They paused and came together, with Meeker saying, "You

know how to get across this part of the Rubys in the dark, Jordan?''

"I'll find it—"

"No, you won't," Meeker said. "You'll go in circles. I know the best way out, and by mornin' we'll be on the other side, lookin' down on the Madison Valley. Then you can go your way."

"I don't want you two in this trouble," Jordan said, looking at the dark outline of Gwen, where she sat on her horse next to him.

"I owe you something," Gwen said, and turned to Meeker. "Get us out of here, Amos."

Suddenly, Jordan heard a rustling in the brush behind, and he turned, snatching out the Winchester from its scabbard on the saddle.

"Hold it!" Meeker said quickly. "Only Misty comin'." He spoke to the dog. "Let's go, you slowpoke. Lead us outa here and over the hills."

Misty woofed and loped ahead, disappearing into the night.

"Does he know how to get out of here?" Jordan asked Meeker.

"He thinks he does," Meeker replied, biting off a chew of tobacco. "Does 'im good to think he's a trail dog, but I'll keep 'im right. Come on!"

Meeker, leading his packhorse, urged his mare ahead as though he were a young man used to the saddle. Jordan grinned to himself and followed. At his side, Gwen rode close at hand, and Jordan looked over, just barely able to see her face in the dark.

"We're even," he said.

She seemed to smile and looked away, saying nothing. Grant Jordan did not know what was in Gwen's mind just then, but even if he had seen the mixed sadness and happiness that mingled there, he would still not have known why she was so confused. To tell the truth, even Gwen herself did not understand the tumult of emotions inside her. All she knew in her mind was that Grant Jordan had a chance to escape military punishment now, and that made her happy. But in her heart, the awareness that he would leave her soon, probably forever, saddened her. But Gwen Quinn was full of a stubborn determination to get on with business. She was too anxious to rescue her father's mine to realize that, in her heart, love for Grant Jordan was growing and was in need of nurturing—the kind of nurturing that could be given only by a woman willing to commit herself to a man. Gwen Quinn was not yet that kind of woman. Maybe she never would be.

They rode through darkness all that night, up a steep trail, then across flat ground that seemed to be a plateau on the top of a mountain. Woods were thick all around, and the crisp air smelled of fresh pine and mossy, moist earth. Jordan's body was still sore from the beating he had taken that afternoon, but his mind was concentrating on what route he would take north.

By now he had learned that Gwen and Meeker had packed all his belongings on his mare, doing so with no one else knowing who had emptied his room in the Chicago House Hotel. He worried about Billy Buchanan. Also, it was possible that Gwen and Amos would be suspected of helping in the escape. But once they split up, it would be difficult to prove they had ever been together. After they got across the mountains, they would go their own ways—Gwen and Meeker down to Greenfield's stage stop on the Madison River and Jordan to buffalo country, riding hard for a few days to leave Virginia City and Captain William Rutledge far behind.

They seldom talked as they went, all of them busy with their thoughts. Meeker knew the ground well. Once or twice they rested the horses at streams, but even then they said little.

Meeker sat and puffed his pipe, keeping his distance from the two of them as though he thought they had some unfinished private business to complete. Gwen sat silently whenever they rested, and Jordan did the same.

Then, about an hour before daybreak, they halted in a cove beneath a cliff that sheltered them from a rising morning wind. They hobbled the horses and wearily slumped down against the rock face. The light of the false dawn gave an illuminating sheen to the world. As usual, Meeker sat apart from them, opening a bag of food and rummaging in it for bread and cheese. Gwen pulled a can of peaches from her own sack, opened it, and handed it to Jordan.

"I owe you one of these, too," she said, and smiled. She was disappointed when he did not smile back. That troubled her. More, it bothered her that she should even care whether this man would smile at her. After all, he had no reason to show her any particular kindness. He had already done so much. Watching Jordan as he drank from the tin, Gwen thought he was nice to look at, even in dim light. He lowered the can and took a deep breath; when he caught her gazing at him, she looked away quickly.

"Am I taking too much?" he asked. "Sorry. You want some?"

"No, no," she said without looking at him, and took another can of peaches from her bag. "I've got one, I was . . . just looking, that's all."

"Oh," he said blankly, thought for a moment, then began to eat the peaches.

Gwen should have been hungry, but she was not. There she sat with an open can of peaches in her hand, but she had no desire to eat any. She felt glum, dull, and annoyed with herself. After a few moments, Jordan said, "We should be goin' on, eh, Amos?" The old-timer took the pipe from his mouth and nodded vaguely. Jordan stood up and stretched.

He was feeling better now. Freedom was something special, and he said so. "Ah, world, it feels good! I tell you, I've never quite been so down as I was cooped up in that shed today! No, sir! Guess it comes from bein' used to freedom, bein' used to comin' and goin' like a man should. Know what I mean?"

Jordan looked down at Gwen, who was not watching him. He saw the peaches still in her hand.

"Hey, you haven't finished. We've a ways to go before we're clear of these hills, and come daybreak, the army'll be out after me. You should eat now while—"

"I know it!" Gwen snapped, and stood up quickly. She walked away, calling softly to her horse, the tin of peaches still in her hand. Then she stared at it, feeling a sudden anger or sadness or frustration—she didn't know what—and threw the can into the darkness, the juice spattering over her as she released it. She began to tremble, and her shoulders seemed to be out of control, jerking up and down, as though she were sobbing, but that could not be! Why should she be sobbing?

"Hey," Jordan said gently, standing beside her. "You all right?"

He put his hand lightly on her back, but she pulled away, saying with a sniff, "I'm okay! Let's go!" She caught her horse and mounted. It was light enough now to see the trail, which cut across an open mountain meadow deep in grass. The faint blush of a red dawn was on the horizon ahead of them.

"Go on, Misty!" Gwen said to the sleepy hound, sending it obediently along the path. Then she rode on, leaving the two men standing beside one another, Jordan confused, Meeker chewing on his pipe stem.

"She all right, Amos?" Jordan asked, watching her move toward the light of dawn.

"Guess not," Amos replied, looking at Jordan as though

he were searching for something on the Southerner's face. Then Meeker grunted to himself and went for his mount and the two packhorses.

"Well," Jordan pressed, "what's wrong? She worried about being caught? Maybe we should split up now, before the army gets close. They might have Indian scouts along, and they could trail us. In daylight, they'd be up this mountain in half the time it took us to pick our way through the dark—"

"Boy," Amos said, and bit the pipe hard as he spoke, "don't you know nothin' about women?"

Jordan stopped and thought a moment. He knew a lot about women, and he was about to say so when Meeker mounted up and began to turn his horse away. Jordan got on the Appaloosa, took the lead rein for his packhorse, and rode up behind Meeker.

"What do you mean? She got woman trouble?"

Meeker shook his head and let out a sigh between his teeth, still clamped on the pipe. "She's got man trouble, son."

Jordan thought about that, let Meeker drift ahead again, then came alongside him once more. "Somebody let her down, Amos?"

Amos gave one short nod.

"No! Why he must be a dumb son of a—"

"That's right, boy. Dumb is the word for it. You're dumb, all right. I ain't seen anybody dumber'n you since I was out in Californy in forty-nine. This feller was so dumb he paid his last nickle for a claim he thought was gonna make his fortune—"

"What did you say?" Jordan could hardly believe what Meeker had just told him. Had he heard right? "Who's a dumb son of a—"

"I'm lookin' at 'im."

"Amos, you got to explain yourself!"

"I guess when them Injun women take a hankerin' to a dude like you, they know it, an' you know it right quick an' kin do what you want about it, no time wasted. But white girls, now, some of the better ones like Missy Quinn here, they don't always know their own mind. Sometimes they take a hankerin' to a drifter like yourself, an' they don't rightly know it themselves, not till the drifter tells 'em, that is, an—"

"Me?" Jordan leaned over to see him better. "You sayin' that girl? . . . Hah!" He tried to laugh it off, but Meeker was speaking again.

". . . an' if the feller cares anythin' about the girl, he won't waste no time in tellin' her that he knows how much she loves 'im—"

"Loves him?"

"But if he don't care for her, then he lets her down easy if he's a gentleman—which I once thought you was—an' he don't tell her that she loves 'im, but he says some nice things that let her down easy, let her down feelin' good, an' feelin' right glad to have knowed a real gentleman, an' feelin'—"

"Amos! What makes you an all-fired expert on women?"

"Got a woman or three myself, son, an' they's the happiest wives I know. Sight happier than that little girl ridin' lonesome up there. Now if I was you—"

"You ain't!" Jordan gave his horse a kick and sent it trotting along ahead of Meeker, but he did not try to catch up with Gwen. Before he would do that, he had some hard thinking to get through.

Chapter 8

Gwen Quinn thought herself a proper fool. She rode ahead into the warm rush of morning that blossomed over the mountaintops, but she saw neither the beauty of the autumn nor the twists and turns her horse followed on the winding trail. Words and sentences came and vanished in her mind, thoughts half formed, quickly rejected by her reason. The struggle within gave her no rest, yet offered no explanation for why she should feel so miserable. Why should she care at all if Grant Jordan went on his way?

No! I won't let myself be distracted from getting back to Pa! I won't let . . . whatever it is I'm feeling for him get in the way of what I have to do. . . . He's got his future laid out for him, and I've got mine. . . .

So went her thoughts, the determination to push on, no matter what, alternating with her longing to ask Jordan to come with her to the mine. She rode with her head down, sometimes with her eyes closed, as she tried to get things clear—to separate the woman in her from the miner's daughter with an obligation to her father. It was not easy, that ride in the dawn, two hours over rough and rocky country, wild and raw, inviting and merciless all at the same time.

Gwen was not a woman to let her emotions fly out of control. She was not a woman to give her heart easily, and in all her twenty-one years, she had never before felt the turmoil of falling so in love with someone who apparently did not love her. This long journey had been difficult, tragic, and it was ending in a way she had never experienced. It was now becoming melancholy, and she did not like it.

In a spirited rush of decision, Gwen made up her mind. She would see to it that whatever she felt for Grant Jordan disappeared from her thoughts. Whatever spell his presence wove around her, she would break it and keep it from enveloping her any further. She knew his heart had no place for her, and that was that. She sniffed and sighed, drawing in breath, shakily at first and then again with strength. It was as though Gwen were inhaling the morning light, finding the capacity to go on, fresh and renewed, as she had felt the day she left Salt Lake City for home with ten thousand dollars in the strongbox.

She reached back and touched the leather satchel that now held the money. This was what counted most. This meant saving her father's sanity, his life. Her father's well-being was contained within this little box, and nothing, nothing at all, would prevent her from giving him the chance to rebuild his life.

The mountains ahead gave way to sky and more sky. The blue reached down lower on the horizon before them, and from behind, she heard Meeker say, "We're almost out of the Rubys. Be lookin' down on the Madison Valley in a minute."

Gwen turned and glanced back, and she was surprised to see Jordan, between her and Meeker, staring right at her in a way that made her spine tingle. She found herself looking back at him, drawn into his eyes as though there were no bottom to the depths of his thoughts. Then Meeker's voice distracted her, and she turned to see that the trail had come out on a ridge. As the old man had predicted, the wide, flat river valley spread in a vast expanse below them.

They paused there, with Misty on his haunches, panting away, the hound looking alternately at Meeker and at the trail leading down the slope to the valley. The river bottom was still green along the meandering banks of the Madison, but the grass blanketing the flats was dry and brown, the color of old hay. Across the plain were the majestic Madisons, some of the peaks rising more than ten thousand feet into the sky. They were bluish in the distance, with the sun off to the east, a little to the right. Now the snowfields scattered over the peaks of the mountains glittered and shone like silver. None of the travelers spoke, for each was overwhelmed by the beauty of the valley and mountain range.

"Good place to be," Jordan said to himself, and Gwen faced him.

"It is," she replied, and gazed off to the south, in the direction of the gold mine. "That's why we're here, Pa and me."

"You aim to stay here?" he asked.

She looked at him and then quickly away before replying, "Why not? It's a good place, as you said. Haven't found any better."

His eyes sought hers.

"I hope you have a good life," she said almost hoarsely, and cleared her throat. Then she forced herself to look at him again and smiled.

They sat on their horses and said nothing as a brisk wind whipped down the valley from the north and blew against them. Meeker had drifted away and dismounted. He was busy with his horse's cinch and talking to Misty, who was sniffing around his jacket pockets for a snack. Jordan and Gwen looked out at the valley in silence, each realizing that parting was nearly upon them, both more aware than ever of a reluctance to leave.

Neither had expected the surge of love that had come so suddenly upon them both—the sharp, quick kind of love that leaves no room for uncertainty or indecision. It was the kind of love that persists, strong and bittersweet, no matter what the lovers want to do with tomorrow. So they sat there, without exchanging words, neither one sure of what was in the other's heart because both were too entangled in the confusion of their own. That was what kept Gwen and Jordan silent and apart, while old Amos Meeker shook his head and spoke quietly to Misty:

"Tell me, pard, were you that foolish when you were young? Ever been in love? No, you're too damn independent yourself. Just like them. You had your mind made up from the start. That's why you hitched up with me, eh? Knew you'd never have to stay in one place long enough to feel guilty about leavin' one day."

Misty snorted and shook his floppy ears. Meeker took a twist of dried beef from his pocket and gave it to the dog. Then he looked up at the couple gazing out at the mountains.

"Time's a wastin'," Meeker said, and mounted up. "You two don't have to say no good-byes till we're down this slope, and that's another fifteen minutes. So plan somethin' out, get it said, and let's have breakfast and be on our ways."

Meeker led them down the rocky trail, steep and treacherous, with Misty lingering behind his horse, the dog picking his own path among boulders and sagebrush. They were near the bottom at a green and overgrown gully when Meeker looked at his pocket watch and said, "We can rest here an hour or so but not much longer. It's eight now, and the army's gonna be through here by noon lookin' for you, Jordan, sure as shootin'."

The glade was centered on a bright, pretty stream, lively and cool, that flowed from the Ruby Mountains and out across the flats toward the Madison River. There were thickets of tall willows and aspen, and stands of spruce, green and well watered, crowded up and down the steep sides of the gully. They unsaddled and hobbled their horses, letting them roam over sweet grass that was a blessing in this dry country. Jordan built a small fire, and Gwen fetched water in the pot for coffee. While the coffee boiled, she brought out a skillet and fried up a mess of bacon and beans. Some day-old bread and tinned fruit were divided on metal plates, and the three of them prepared for their last meal together.

But first Jordan got clean clothes and moved a short distance away into the shelter of some willows, finding a deeper pool there, stripping naked, and immersing himself in the cold water. It was bracing, even painful for his bruises, but by the time he came out, he felt fresh and strong again. As he dressed, the scent of Gwen's meal came to him, a good fragrance, comfortable and relaxing.

Then Misty growled. Jordan was buttoning his shirt when the dog began to bark, his nose aimed up the trail, which was visible for two hundred yards as it snaked over the side of the slope. Jordan thought the dog might have sensed a bear, and he scanned the hill while tugging on his boots. Grizzlies were common in this country, and dangerous. Then he heard, like distant bells, the clink and clatter of a cavalryman's field gear, and he knew he had blundered. Soldiers were coming! He dashed out of the thicket toward his friends, who were both anxiously looking up the slope, where nothing showed as yet. Without speaking, Jordan snatched up his saddle and guns. Gwen watched him, fear in her eyes.

"I'll take cover back in the trees," he said quickly. "Don't get too deep in this. If it gets difficult, say you met me on the road and I lit out when I saw the soldiers come down the hill.''

Gwen and Meeker watched as Jordan caught his Appaloosa, leaving the mare to graze, and he led the horse into the brush, where the two of them vanished like ghosts. Gwen and Meeker looked at each other, she feeling an empty burning inside her, finding it hard to breathe. Gwen caught her breath and swallowed, willing herself to be calm. But her heart was thumping. Misty was woofing and starting up the slope, challenging the sounds that were nearly at the crest above.

"Have some breakfast," Meeker said, and winked at her. "We better get to it afore it burns. One thing I hate is burned beans, specially when an army patrol interrupts the eatin' of 'em." He emptied Jordan's plate into his own.

With that, they sat about looking casual, ladling the food out, pouring strong, black coffee, and finding seats on a cottonwood trunk that lay nearby. Gwen's mouth was dry, and she had no appetite, but she forced the food down. She was grateful for the wind that blew into the gully from the flats, for it cooled her, and she hoped her face would not be too flushed when the soldiers came down.

The patrol appeared up the trail, and it was only a few minutes until they reached the bottom, moving leisurely, the leader taking his time to search out the scene around him. There were twelve soldiers, led by Lieutenant Wilkinson, and there were two Pawnee Indian scouts with them. It was these two no doubt who had trailed them. Lanterns hung from their saddles.

Meeker glanced swiftly at Gwen as if to be sure of her own composure, then rose to meet the soldiers. They drew up and stopped, the horses tossing their heads at the smell of fresh water. The soldiers were dusty and worn, obviously having traveled through the night and traveled hard. Wilkinson looked tense as he motioned for the Pawnee scouts to dismount and examine the area. Gwen barely restrained a gasp as she saw them make a direct line along Jordan's path and disappear into the same thicket as he did.

Wilkinson touched his hat to Gwen and leaned forward in the saddle before he said deliberately and with a tone of warning in his voice, "You both know why we're here, of course."

Meeker was lighting his pipe. He squinted through the smoke, puffed a few times, and said, "Yep. Reckon army horses need a drink now and again. Why don't you set a spell. We'll share this here water with your boys, Lieutenant. Looks like you've had a long night of it."

Wilkinson's jaw tightened, and his jowls twitched. He glared at Meeker before saying, "If you have any sense, old man, you won't get any further involved in this than you already have. Where's Jordan?"

Meeker puffed and took the pipe out of his mouth. He eyed the lieutenant for a moment. "You mean you came all the way out here, ridin' through the night, riskin' government horses, an' you ain't certain if he's here or not?"

Gwen felt her legs tremble. She drank coffee and was surprised it did not spill, for her hands were almost shaking. Did Wilkinson see it? The officer sat back in the saddle, turned to his men, and told them to dismount and water their horses. As the troopers got down, all of them bone weary and in bad moods, Wilkinson gave a scornful grin and said slowly, "You've been warned, both of you."

Then the soldiers gathered near the stream, a man taking charge of Wilkinson's mount. The lieutenant moved away and wearily sank down on some bunchgrass, entering into conversation with a corporal, who pointed now and again in the direction the Indian scouts had gone. Gwen did not like it when she saw Wilkinson take off his hat and smile confidently, nodding and looking at the thicket where the Indians were hunting for their quarry.

Up among the rocks and trees, Jordan had seen the Indians come after him. There was nothing he could do, nowhere to go. He had hoped to hide, though he had realized crafty Pawnee trackers might be along with the patrol. Now he was standing in a scrub growth of head-high sagebrush mingled with cedars that gave good cover from the soldiers below. He could see the men dismount and rest their horses, but they could not see him. As long as the Appaloosa—saddled now— remained quiet, he might not be detected. He held his hand over the animal's nose, speaking soothingly to it now and again. But all the while, his insides churned, for he did not know where those Pawnees were. And what would he do if they found him? Would he fight? Would he take on the entire patrol? That would be foolish—

The horse stamped and whickered nervously. Jordan sensed something, too. He whirled quickly, and there, less than twenty yards away, stood the two Pawnee scouts, rifles in hand, staring at him. Neither solemn brave showed the slightest emotion. Jordan faced them, showing no emotion, either. His rifle was leaning against a tree close by, but in that explosive moment, he knew he did not want to kill anyone. The two scouts were still staring at him, their eyes dark and unfathomable. Jordan stilled his horse, returned their gaze, and waited.

Then, as though with one accord, the Pawnees turned quickly and vanished in the shadows of the trees, gone as silently as they had appeared. Jordan knew they were heading back to the patrol. Apparently, they did not want to risk a gunfight without the support of the other soldiers. Perhaps they had orders from Wilkinson to locate him and then return because Wilkinson wanted the honor of taking him . . . or perhaps the lieutenant had something else in mind, something lethal that involved evening the score with Jordan. His insides knotted, and he felt embittered to have been snared like this.

He spoke to his horse, and the animal quieted down. There was nothing to do now but wait and calculate his path when he had to make a break for it. He did not want to fight the soldiers, but if Wilkinson gave him no other choice . . .

After a few moments, he saw through the trees that the two scouts had returned. They were walking to Wilkinson, who listened and turned his gaze up the slope now and again. Then Jordan looked at Gwen, who was on her feet, intent on the officer. Jordan found himself strangely more interested in watching Gwen at that moment, unconcerned with Wilkinson for an instant. She was a fine-looking woman, that was sure. She stood her ground well while Wilkinson was so close at hand, and Jordan admired her more than ever.

Then Jordan's attention was caught by the quick movement of the soldiers. The scouts were heading for their horses, and Wilkinson was stamping among his men, angrily urging them to mount up. What was happening now? Were they going to charge up here, mounted? Wilkinson was very likely the kind who would do just that, risking the lives of his men for the sake of drama.

But Jordan was bewildered by what happened next. The patrol thundered down through the gulch, heading for the flats, away from where Jordan was hidden. They were moving off at a rapid clip, Wilkinson and the scouts at the head, as though the man they were hunting had already escaped and was fleeing northward! Jordan watched, amazed, as the soldiers whirled down the gulch in a cloud of dust and moved out onto the flats, making a small thin line of dark blue against the brown grass. In a moment, they were half a mile away, heading northwest, parallel with the Ruby Range, keeping close to the foot of the hills.

Jordan shook his head, gave a little chuckle, and led his horse back down the slope, his rifle in hand. He was ready to go, but now he was uncertain just which direction to take. The soldiers were now ahead of him if he wanted to ride north. As he moved through the brush, he looked down to see Gwen standing close to Meeker, both of their faces turned to him. He pulled the Appaloosa on, urging it to follow, but it seemed to have its own ideas and was slow to come with him.

"Don't you be difficult now, Injun! I got enough to trouble my thinkin' without you actin' up. Come on! Come on, now!" He pondered what was next, and before he broke through the cover and approached Gwen and Meeker, he had made up his mind.

But it took him by surprise when Gwen rushed at him, tears in her eyes, and threw her arms around him, her breathing quick and anxious. He held Gwen close to hush her, and she felt very good. Then he eased her back and looked down at her, losing himself in her beauty.

Meeker said, "You must have some cousins among the Pawnee, brother."

Jordan looked at him, then at Gwen, then back at Amos again. "What happened?"

Gwen said, "The scouts claimed you'd slipped out at the lower end of the gully." She laughed. "They told Wilkinson that you were not far ahead, and you were on the way north! They convinced Wilkinson he could catch you if he moved fast!" She laughed again and bit her lip, her eyes shining.

"Well," Jordan said, and grinned at Gwen, "looks like I can't go north, doesn't it?"

"Looks that way," she almost whispered, and stared at him, keen and hopeful. Jordan saw that look of hope again, the hope he had recognized in Gwen's eyes when first they met. That look was very appealing to him just then.

He said to Amos, "Old-timer, how far are we from Greenfield's stage station?"

"Six hours if we don't stop every time you feel like runnin' off in the brush!"

Jordan took Gwen by the shoulders. "I guess I would like to see that gold mine of yours, after all."

Gwen had tears coming again, and once more she felt a fool. But it was a wonderful kind of foolishness, indeed!

They rode hard until late in the afternoon, heading south along the flats, keeping close to the base of the hills—not so easy to see in case a stray party of hostiles or another patrol was roving the countryside. As they went, Jordan thought of those two Pawnee scouts and understood they were repaying him for trying to stop the attack on Hoko-lana's people. Once more, he thought of that tragedy, and he wondered where Kintara and the braves who had fled with him were. If Kintara had not been a hostile before, he certainly would be now.

As the three of them made their way through the Madison Valley, with a stiff wind blowing steadily at their backs, Jordan could not help feeling they were being watched. To the right above them, the Rubys rose bleak and gray, with green clumps of fir and pine and a few stands of cottonwood where streams ran down. The hills were bare and desolate, but Jordan found himself jerking around in the saddle now and again to look at them, searching for some movement that would reveal a spy following. His instinct in such things was always good, so he was certain they were being observed. Meeker noticed his restlessness, but neither man spoke of it.

The sun was beginning to drop toward evening when they brought in sight the squat log ranch house that was their destination. Greenfield's station stood on a little rise above the river, with a few shade trees towering over the place. As they came closer, they saw a small barn, a few sheds, and two corrals. There were plenty of horses in the corrals, indicating that stage teams were kept on hand here, but as hard as Jordan looked, he could see no stagecoach anywhere on the grounds.

Gwen was thinking the same. The sturdy house sat apart from the outbuildings, and she searched every part of the place as they approached, but it was obvious that no coach was there. Apprehension grew in her. They drew up in front of the station, and Misty found himself surrounded by a pack of two-month-old puppies that leaped all around him as though he were their long-lost father. The black and white pups yelped and yapped with boundless energy, while Misty stood calm and bored, his head swiveling slowly from side to side, taking in the surroundings.

As the newcomers dismounted, the door of the house opened, and out came a large, barrel-chested man in shirt-sleeves who raised his chin and peered at them a minute before recognizing Gwen.

"Ah, Miss Quinn," said Horace Greenfield, snapping his suspenders and hiking up his trousers. His sleeves were rolled up, and his face was friendly and well fed. "Thought you'd be gettin' here about this time. Your supplies arrived this mornin', an' the boys who hauled 'em stored 'em out in the barn. You'll see everythin's in order, and I have a packing slip that they signed, so it's all official—"

"Mr. Greenfield, is there a stagecoach for us?" Gwen needed that answer quickly.

"Well, now." Greenfield rubbed his big hands together and nodded slowly. "Well, let's see. Party from Canada went out two days ago on the tour for Yellowstone Park, an' if they make it through the Indians—damn fools they were, an'

I had 'em put down a big deposit to guarantee the stage being replaced if they got their hair lifted—as I was sayin', if they didn't have no trouble with Indians, then they ought to be back two weeks next Tuesday, that's—''

"Two weeks!" Gwen was horrified. After all she had done . . . By then, it could snow, and the mine's access road would be blocked. Her heart sank as she realized plainly she was on the brink of failure.

Meeker spoke. "What the hell are tourists doin' takin' a coach through hostile territory an' goin' up into the mountains this time of year when snow could hit any time?''

Greenfield just shook his head. "Danged if I can figure them tourists out; they go clean ahead of me. But ever since the government made all that country up around the Tetons into a park a few years back, I seen more tourists come through here than a fox has fleas. Yep, it ain't like the old days when it was a man's country . . . no offense intended, Miss Quinn . . . no, not at all. Them tourists come with ladies, an' the ladies got umberellays an' hoop skirts and lap dogs, an' how they do complain when they get here an' find out there ain't no hotel, when the tour book they bought back East tells 'em there is. Shucks! There ain't never been a hotel here since the Blackfeet burned down my pa's old inn, an' then that was only a place for miners an' cowmen an' hunters, not tourists. . . .''

Greenfield went on about tourists, but Gwen heard nothing of what he said. Without a fast-moving stage, there was no way she could get the supplies and dynamite up to the mine quickly. The best they could do would be to hire a wagon and get there in ten days or so. But when she got a word in to ask Greenfield about a wagon, he said there weren't any for hire and that all he had was a rickety hay wagon that never went more than a mile or two from the station. Not even a wagon!

Gwen looked at her friends, who were standing near their

horses as the animals drank from the trough. In the back of her mind, she heard the stage owner rambling on about wagons and Indians and tourists, but for the rest she felt numb, helpless. Jordan looked at her, concerned, but without an answer as to how the supplies, dynamite, and payroll would get up to the mine before snow blocked the way.

Greenfield was speaking. "It's a bad time to try to go through, Miss Quinn, though I know how your pa must need supplies for the winter; but them hostiles is awful bad! Awful bad! Nothin' has tried to go up that way since the freight wagons were attacked weeks ago, an' I wouldn't like to try it myself. Even horsemen are in danger headin' up that way, to my thinkin'."

But Gwen had already decided to ride on horseback up to the mine with the payroll. That way the miners could be paid and would stay the winter. Perhaps Meeker would wait here until a wagon or a stage was available, then bring on the dynamite and supplies. If she could, Gwen would ride back with a few miners to help bring the supplies through. But before she could take her friends aside and lay out her plan, Amos Meeker said to Greenfield, "You got no coach, but would you sell us some of that horseflesh?"

Greenfield thought a moment, feeling at the stubble on his chin. He eyed Meeker and said, "For the right price, friend, I'll sell the whole place."

"Don't want the place," Meeker said, looking at Gwen for her agreement. "Just two span o' good pullers. I want a smart leader, and they all have to be good in the mountains."

Gwen nodded to Meeker, not knowing what he had in mind but willing to let him try anything at all. Since they had no coach, Greenfield was confused, but if there was money to be made, he would go along with them. He and his two hired hands led Meeker to the corral, where the old man picked out four horses after checking each one closely, looking at their

mouths for telltale signs of calluses or bruises that revealed
they had been badly used by a driver who reined them too
tightly. Hard-mouthed horses were spoiled for a skillful reinsman who controlled a team with only the lightest touch of the
leathers.

Half an hour later, after Jordan and Gwen had grained the
horses and thrown together a quick, cold meal in the kitchen
of the ranch, Meeker came back, saying to Greenfield as they
approached, "Your drivers must know their business, friend.
Them animals got real sweet mouths, good stock."

"Indeed they do." Greenfield was pleased that Meeker,
who obviously had much knowledge about stage teams, was
so complimentary. All the while, Gwen and Jordan were in
the dark about Meeker's plans. But they went along with
him, and Gwen paid a fair price for the horses, which were
strung together and led out of the station, Meeker going first.
As they rode away, Greenfield shouted another warning about
Indians and cried out that Gwen's supplies would be safe in
his barn until they came back.

They rode westward into the beginnings of sunset, toward
the Rubys again. Two hours later, they entered the mouth of
a draw that Jordan would have sworn was not there as they
first approached it. A crowd of trees and an outcropping of
rock concealed the ravine, and it was a perfect place for a
hideout, Jordan thought. As they rode, he called to Meeker,
"When you gonna let us in on your secret, Amos?"

Meeker looked back over his shoulder and said, "Any
minute now, Johnny Reb. An' you, Missy Quinn, you kin get
that sad look off yer face, 'cause everythin'll be all right.
Wait an' see, girlie." He grinned at Gwen, and she straight-
ened up in the saddle. But her back was sore, her legs ached,
and she was too depressed to think much past the next step of
her horse. This would be the last hope—whatever Meeker
was planning. If it was all wrong, she would ride out at

dawn, with or without Jordan at her side, to take the money to her father. They went into the draw, which inclined upward a little but was fairly smooth, open ground.

At the top of the bluff, above them to the left, a steep tower of rock was dark against the sky, a good landmark for anyone needing to remember this place. That, surely, was Meeker's sign telling him where the ravine was hidden in all the rugged tumble of the Rubys. Jordan was silent, wondering what their next move would be. Like Gwen, he had faith in old Amos, and he would keep his peace until the old man had his show.

The ravine was thickly wooded on the left, and a brook ran through it there. Light was fading from the sky, and in the west, the colors of sunset—pink and yellow and lavender— were gathering in strength. Meeker rode right up to a steep cliff, which had dense undergrowth at its base, and then dismounted.

"Here we be," he said with a cheerfulness that the others did not share. It was as though the old prospector was growing in strength as adversity increased. Jordan liked the man, but he had no idea why they were here at the wrong end of a box canyon.

Gwen felt the same. She was in no mood for games, and especially not for further disappointment. Meeker led the team of horses off to one side and hitched their halter ropes to a tree. His own horse stood with grounded reins.

"Well, git down, you two! Show a little spunk! An' mind yer manners; yer about to meet Arabella!" He tugged a hatchet from his packhorse.

Gwen remembered the name Arabella from Virginia City. The jaded lady. Jordan, amused and puzzled, got down from his horse. Seeing how tired Gwen was, he helped her dismount as Meeker began to chop and tear at the undergrowth with the hatchet. For a brief moment, Jordan stood with his hands at her waist. Gwen, looking up at him, seemed so very tired and dismal. He was about to say something encouraging when suddenly Meeker shouted, "Give me a hand there, boy. Come here!"

Jordan went to him and was surprised to see that the undergrowth covered what appeared to be a fair-sized shed. As he helped Meeker pull away the branches and some tumbleweed, he asked, "What the hell's Arabella doin' in here? Is she dead or alive?"

Meeker tugged at the last foliage and with the hatchet handle knocked away a peg jamming the double doors shut.

"I said mind yer manners, and I meant it!" Meeker said, though not too harshly. "Arabella ain't dead. But she's just waitin' to be born again, as them preachers say. Well, this child's gonna reborn 'er. She's been waitin' here for me." He hauled at the door, which scraped slowly over the dirt, creaking and groaning as he pulled. Gwen was behind them now, interested and watching everything. She gasped when Meeker opened the hidden shed. Inside was a stagecoach set up on cottonwood blocks!

"Meet Arabella!" Meeker beamed, resting his hand on the coach pole, which looked like new. In fact, the whole coach looked as though it were in perfect condition. It had been painted before being put up on blocks, and everything about it told of expert care and much affection.

"Arabella!" Gwen gasped, running her hands along the side of the coach. It had no doors on its side openings, and its wheel rims were wider than a Concord passenger coach. This was, she knew, what was called a mud wagon. But a mud wagon was no term of insult; instead, it meant that it was built to go even through mud and could travel almost anywhere. Furthermore, a mud wagon was built for speed, not for passenger comfort. The best of them were very fast.

All these things Meeker told them as they carefully knocked

out the lift blocks and set the coach on its wheels. As they dragged it out into the sunlight, Meeker said he had driven this coach for three years on a run between Salt Lake City and Helena. But the small line he worked for had been forced under by the Overland Stage Company, owned by the unscrupulous Ben Holladay. When Meeker's employer could not pay him the four months' wages owed just before the company closed its doors, the man gave him the stage—called Arabella by Meeker, who regarded it the way a cowboy loved a fine cutting horse.

"Well," said Meeker as they stood around admiring the stage, and Misty snuffed at it, wagging his tail in recognition, "I hadn't no use for a coach, and I hadn't no use for the few hundred dollars I could have sold her for, and I sure didn't want to part with her right off, so I just slipped her in that shed there—I used to have a cabin here once, but it burned down, all but the shed. An' Arabella's been like money in the bank, so to speak. If'n I was really desperate for cash, I'd have come for her an' sold her, but even though I was mighty tight now an' then, I was never that mighty tight. So here's Arabella, Missy Quinn, an' this little lady'll prove what she can do."

Meeker was aglow with happiness and pride as he showed every detail of the mud wagon. He pointed out the sturdy running gear, saying it needed some greasing and general care before they left, and as Gwen, giggling, climbed inside to look over the load capacity, Meeker assured her that all the supplies could be carried inside, on top, and in the boot.

He chuckled and said, "When we pull into Greenfield's tomorrow, won't that farmer's eyes bug out! Hah! An' when this run's over, I might just go into the tourist-freightin' business myself after winter. Yes, sir, Arabella's the quickest, handiest, downright spunkiest lady in the territory—'ceptin' you, Missy Quinn, if you get my meanin'."

Gwen jumped out and threw her arms around Meeker, giving him a huge hug. "Oh, Amos!" She knew at last that they really had a chance to get through with everything her father needed. All she had fought for, and all her cousins had died for, could be achieved now!

"Amos, Amos!" She laughed and wept all at the same time, and Jordan grinned as Meeker looked over the girl's shoulder and winked at him. Jordan felt good, too, but he would have felt far better if he did not still have the haunting impression that they were being watched.

Chapter 9

For two hours, they worked hard, applying grease to the running gear, oiling the harnesses, and cleaning dust that after several years had covered every part of the coach. Gwen even polished the two brass coal-oil lamps fixed at the sides of the stage, and Jordan had not seen her look so happy. She worked as hard as the men did, and when it was almost dark, they stood back and looked at Arabella gleaming in the failing light of early evening.

"She's just beautiful!" Gwen said contentedly. "She's just beautiful, Amos! No wonder you kept her so long. I never thought I'd say that sort of thing about an old stagecoach, but my, she looks fine!"

Meeker, like Jordan, was spattered with black grease. "Indeed she do look fine! Finer than I remembered. An' she goes as she looks, slick and nifty! No Injun's gonna have it easy runnin' us to ground, no, siree!"

Jordan looked at Meeker, liking what the man was saying. No doubt Amos could drive as well as Arabella looked. Jordan found himself smiling as he looked the stage over, marking its oval shape, curved sides, thin and marvelously crafted. He took stock of its strong, almost indestructible wheels. He had heard about Concord mud wagons, and he knew Meeker was not boasting with empty words when he said Arabella could go. Likely, with those four good horses hitched to her, Meeker would make Arabella fairly fly.

Jordan contemplated Gwen, who was wiping smeared dirt from her face with a rag. She stared back at him, hesitated, then smiled. Meeker, self-conscious but happy, slipped away, leaving them alone, muttering about scrounging some firewood if they would clean up and get ready to cook dinner. Misty drifted away, too, and they both melted into the shadows.

Jordan and Gwen were still looking at one another as Meeker's last words gave way to silence. Her eyes were big and peaceful; his were intent and searching. Then they were standing close together, facing the stagecoach. They stayed that way for a while until Gwen said, "Life is strange, isn't it?"

On an impulse, Jordan moved to her, and when he brought up his oily hands to take hers, he jumped back quickly and let go. But it was too late. Her hands were filthy now, and she laughed about it. He apologized, half laughing himself. Then she suddenly rubbed grease on his face, and he grabbed her wrists, drawing her against him. Gwen gave in a little, and he felt her yield. Her eyes were closed, expecting his kiss, but instead he rubbed his dirty cheek against her face, and she yelped, throwing him back, both of them laughing.

Gwen cleaned the grease from her face with a rag and said, "Don't think you'll get another chance like that to kiss me."

Jordan smiled and came to her, but she backed off, her eyes mischievous. "I mean it," she said, smirking. "You had your chance. . . ."

She was slipping around behind the stage, Jordan closing in on her; then she darted around it, running to the other side.

But as she ran past, he dived through the other door of the coach, and his hand shot through the near door and caught her wrist again. He was lying prone on the floor of the stage, and he yanked her toward him, getting a grip on her other arm and holding her with both hands. But he had nothing to secure himself, and Gwen dragged him bodily from the coach until his legs flopped to the ground. He threw himself at her, and they tumbled to the ground in a laughing jumble of arms and legs. And then he was beside her, she laughing, he now serious, lying against her, his face close to hers. She stopped laughing and then looked at him with the same searching, serious eyes.

After a moment, she said, "When's the last time you were really happy?"

Jordan gazed at her a moment before saying, "My mind's on something else."

"What?" She wiped a little of the grease from his face.

"You." He did not smile, and his eyes did not waver from hers.

She said, "Why don't you stop thinking and kiss me?"

He did, hard and long, then more gently, and at last with a tenderness that set Gwen's heart to pounding. Her arms were around him, and he lay against her, holding her as though he never wanted to let go. Then, after a moment of joy, they parted, and Gwen saw Jordan's eyes—afire but still harboring something distant. She wished he would speak as they lay there, but she knew he would not.

"I . . . I love you." Her words were hard coming but harder to keep unsaid.

His eyes softened, and he propped his head on his hand, his elbow resting on the ground. "Gwen, I'm not the man for a woman like you to love. . . . Do you understand that?" He knew what his heart was insisting, but for too long Grant Jordan had been in absolute control of his heart and his emotions. Because this girl meant so much to him, he knew he had to maintain that control. He would not hurt her. Now, when he spoke to Gwen, it was not from his heart but from a will that had chosen a drifter's life. "You need someone solid, someone who'll stay with—"

"Have I asked you for anything, Grant?" She did not want to hear him speak like this. She sat up and brought her knees to her chin. "I'm not asking you to be anything you can't:"

Then she felt a little annoyed with herself that this was all becoming so serious. "Hey," she said with an insolent look in her eyes, "you sure get big ideas just because I asked you for a kiss—"

"You just told me you loved me," he said, lying back and snatching a piece of grass to chew on.

She looked over her shoulder. "That's 'cause it was a nice kiss."

He grabbed for her then, his face alight, but she got up quickly and shook out her hair. She gave him a long, questioning stare. He lay back and watched her, thinking how beautiful she was and trying not to consider all the other things he liked so much about Gwen Quinn. It was precisely because he liked her—maybe "like" was not a strong enough word, but it would serve—because he cared about her, that he did not want to push this too much further. He would not take advantage of a girl who might regret it when he moved on, as surely she would. And he surely was going on as soon as he saw her safely to the mine.

Gwen looked down at him, her face shining with the silky colors of early evening. She understood what Jordan had said to her, and as much as she wanted to resist the feeling, she was even more attracted to him now. But Gwen was not the kind to give herself to a drifter who infatuated her. Or so she thought. So until Grant Jordan had something permanent in mind between them, she, too, would stop everything right here. But as they walked back to where Meeker had started a bright campfire a little ways from the stream, she had to smile. It really was, she thought, a very nice kiss.

Before dawn, Meeker and Jordan caught the horses and hitched them to the stage. Meeker was anxious to give the team the feeling of the harness and coach, and he was anxious to get the old feeling back himself. While Jordan readied breakfast, saddled and loaded the other horses, Meeker offered to take Gwen on the stage. Jordan was impressed with Amos's assurance and finesse from the moment the old man climbed into the driver's box. From the shed, Meeker had produced a magnificent black whip, eight feet long, with silver worked onto the handle.

"Pappy gave it to me when I was startin' out," Meeker told them, explaining that his father had been a professional coachman and had taught him the trade. "I used this tickler ever since, had it repaired, refitted, and rewound, but she's the very same. Never nicked a horse yet, though I come close to a lazy one's ear now an' then."

As Meeker started the team, he seemed a statue up in the box. Unlike the savage, gruff Hawk Devlin, who had been killed while driving the first stagecoach, Meeker hardly said a word to his horses even though he did not know them well yet. His hands, holding the reins in his lap, barely moved at all. Watching from her seat next to Amos, Gwen knew the technique was to hold the eight reins separated in pairs between the fingers, signaling the horses by walking the proper fingers along the reins of the horse the driver wanted. That gathered in the leather and put a little pressure against that animal's bit—to one side or the other or evenly—and the horse responded by turning or slowing. Coordinated slackening and gathering in the reins was how the reinsman controlled the team, and it took long years of practice before anyone could become good at it. In his right hand, Meeker also held the whip. Without releasing control of the reins, Meeker gave a clever snap of his wrist—Gwen could not figure out just how—and cracked that long black snake over the head of a horse that wasn't pulling correctly. He did this without losing his sensitive grip on the four reins in that hand, and Gwen was amazed to watch him perform. Hawk Devlin had been all snarl and bluster as he drove his team, but Amos Meeker was quiet and gentle with the horses, never raising his voice until they came back up the ravine to where Jordan was bent over the fire. Then Meeker called a firm "Ho!" to the team, pulled back on the reins, and tramped down hard on the foot brake to bring the stage to a sudden, rocking stop.

Gwen brushed back hair that had blown over her face and said, "You certainly know your business, don't you?"

Meeker just smiled a little and switched the pipe from one side of his mouth to the other. "It's a good team," he said, and they climbed down, both hungry, and eager for the coming journey. For the moment, the dangers and the sorrows were forgotten, and they dug into a good meal of pan bread, bacon, and beans. As usual, Jordan had his tins of peaches, and Gwen found she was beginning to like them better.

They sat around the fire, absorbing its warmth, for the mountain air was chill, and a frost glistened on the grass and trees. But it was not the morning air that made Jordan feel uncomfortable as Gwen and Meeker ate their breakfasts heartily. The nagging feeling that someone was observing them had not left him. It had kept him awake much of the night. While Gwen and Meeker had slept deeply, undisturbed, Jordan had lain with his hand near the Winchester, his body drifting into sleep only from time to time. Misty had been uneasy, too, and Jordan had taken notice whenever the dog had lifted his head to let a low growl roll in his throat.

But despite missing sleep, Jordan had marked nothing. As they finished breakfast, he kept his Winchester by his side and frequently let his eyes rove over the ridges around them, not seeing anything in particular but sure in his blood that someone was out there.

Gwen watched him, but he seemed not to notice her. After a while, Meeker again observed Jordan's restlessness.

"What is it?" Meeker asked him.

Jordan shook his head before replying. "Maybe nothing. Maybe something. I don't know, but I think we're being watched."

Gwen felt her throat constrict, and she swallowed without meaning to. She looked around the ridges herself, but all she saw were the shadows of morning lying on gray rocks in a world that was bleak and dull on the side hidden from the sun and warm and rosy on the side facing the dawn.

Meeker nodded and took a last forkful of beans. "I thought the same. Somebody's been there since the army patrol passed. But it ain't army scouts, that's sure. More like Injuns."

Gwen asked, "Are we in danger?"

Jordan said, "Always in danger if a buck decides to take a shot at us from cover. I can't tell how many there are out there, but I think, Amos, we ought to take the sneakiest way up to the mine—if there is one."

Amos nodded and gathered in the plates and cups to wash them in the stream. "I don't know but two ways to cross the big gorge between here an' there. The way I'm thinkin' of has a natural bridge—a sandstone arch, it is. At least it used to be there—never can tell about them natural bridges. It might be down by now, an' I don't aim to go 'round about that way and find it's been washed out. It's a tough way to go and a tougher way to come back if the bridge ain't there no more.''

Gwen said quickly, "Greenfield would know!''

Amos agreed. ''That he would, Missy Quinn. When we go back for the dynamite and supplies this mornin', we'll find out from him. If the Injuns are watchin' an' think we're goin' up to Tom's mine, they'll be layin' for us on the main route, probably at the new wooden bridge over the gorge. But if we can take the road that jumps the gorge by the natural arch, then we might git through afore they have the time to git goin' an' light out after us. Whoever's skulkin' in these hills won't know which road we're takin' till we reach the fork, an' he won't git to his war party afore we can git across the arch an' be on our way to the mine with the Injuns behind us. But it's a hard road to that arch—rock face on one side an' a straight drop five hundred feet down on the other.''

They hurried to break camp, all of them feeling the tension now. Gwen kicked sand over the fire, and they loaded their gear with Misty into the stage. The packhorses, left unburdened, were tethered to the coach along with Gwen's and Meeker's saddle horses. Gwen and Amos climbed into the box, and Jordan mounted the Appaloosa. He kept his Winchester out and sat facing the hills, bright with sunlight now. Meeker gave the horses a word, cracked his whip, and the team lunged ahead, throwing Gwen back a little, and she grabbed for her hat. She looked down at Jordan, who was staring at the hills, rifle butt on his thigh. Then he turned his big horse and trotted after the stage. Seeing Gwen watching him, he smiled—for the first time that day.

Nothing more had been said about the previous night. Jordan had his mind on whoever was spying on them, and Gwen's thoughts were directed to getting on with her mission. She turned away from Jordan, who was riding alongside, and thought of what they had planned: first to Greenfield's for the cargo, then south toward the southern Madisons and the far side of Koch Peak. She was not familiar with the route Meeker would take over the natural bridge, but as she thought about the main road to the mine, she realized that there were too many good places for attackers to strike—as they had struck her first stage in the bloody ravine on the Beaverhead. She shuddered as she remembered that terrible day, and she tried not to think of her cousins.

"You cold, missy?" Meeker called.

She smiled weakly and shook her head. Then she looked down at Jordan again and felt safe, secure, with him near. As they cut out of the canyon and swept into the grasslands of the Madison Valley, his eyes were often to the rear, still seeking out some sign of an enemy hiding there.

They traveled farther out in an easterly direction into the valley, and Jordan kept glancing behind. Gwen spent much of her time watching Jordan, and Meeker was quiet, content to have the reins in his hands and Arabella speeding along once more. The ground was dry but not too dusty, so Misty could poke his nose out of the stage window and see the world go by. It was a couple of hours to Greenfield's, and Meeker was not pushing the team, knowing there would be no other horses to exchange for them when they tired. He intended to run them easily for two hours at a time, giving them a half-hour break in between. Every four hours, he would unharness them and let them graze. There was no other way to make them last, and Meeker intended to keep the horses as fresh as possible in case Indians appeared and they had to run for it.

Meeker told Gwen they would make the mine at noon the next day. That meant traveling eight hours that day at five miles an hour over flat river bottom on a well-worn road. They had to ford the Madison eventually, but it was shallow this time of year. After sleeping that night, they would then cut eastward up into the foothills, taking the fork of the old road Meeker knew, then crossing a deep gorge spanned by the sandstone arch—if Greenfield said the arch was still there. Much of that journey would be on the crest of a high ridge and, later on, the brink of precipices—dangerous ground for a horseman, let alone a stage.

As Gwen thought about the route, Jordan lingered behind, watching the receding Rubys, now a mile behind them. Then he saw something. He took the field glasses from their carrying case on his saddle and brought them up, stopping the horse as he focused. There, moving down from the hills, was an Indian. Through the binoculars, he looked like a Crow, carrying a rifle and decked out in war feathers. That's who was following them—likely a scout for a larger party. The brave was keeping his distance, but he was tailing them, sure enough. As Meeker said, as soon as this Indian knew they were taking a cutoff rather than following the main road up to Quinn's mine, he would undoubtedly ride for his cronies. Jordan put the binoculars away and galloped after the stagecoach.

When they arrived, Horace Greenfield was amazed to see a coach. With the help of the astonished keeper's hostlers, they loaded the dynamite and supplies. Soon there was barely enough headroom for Misty to lie in the crowded compartment, and ropes were slung across the doors and windows to keep the cargo from sliding out. Before they left, they confirmed with Greenfield that the sandstone bridge on the cutoff road still stood; but, he said, it was weak, and no one with any sense would dare to use it these days. Not even a horseman should risk crossing it, he said, and added bluntly that they were fools if they tried to take a stagecoach over it. Especially, he said, such a handsome coach. Ask as he might, he did not learn how Amos came by the stage.

Meeker thanked Greenfield for his counsel and climbed back into the stagecoach. Gwen came up to his left side and noticed something bulging from his jacket.

"What's that?" she asked as Meeker snapped the whip and the stage pulled out, with Greenfield and his employees standing watching them go.

He grinned and opened the jacket, revealing three sticks of dynamite tucked into his belt. Gwen gasped when she saw them. The fuses were already in place, making them look like giant firecrackers.

"Ain't no better medicine for Injun ailments than this, Missy Quinn. No, siree! Can you throw one if I'm drivin'?"

Gwen could not answer that, and she went pale to think whether she could light a stick of dynamite and throw it. She really did not know the answer at all. Jordan, riding nearby, looked up at Gwen and said, "It'll be easier to handle that dynamite than it would be to handle the team if Amos had to throw a stick. And a lot safer, too."

She was embarrassed at being fainthearted and thought about offering her place in the box to Jordan, willing to ride alongside herself. But she summoned her courage and sat up straight, not replying to Jordan, looking ahead at the rutted trace rather than letting him see her dread.

It was only an hour later that three horsemen rode into Greenfield's. Their leader was Jess Clum, who knew Greenfield well, for his wagons often stopped there to rest on the journey between Salt Lake City and Bozeman up at the north end of the valley of the Madison. Clum was warmly welcomed.

The freight-line owner accepted Greenfield's offer to come in and have coffee, and their conversation quickly turned to a discussion of the Crow troubles. It did not take long for Clum to ask about Gwen Quinn and whether she might have passed through. Greenfield talked readily, telling about Amos Meeker's fine stagecoach, and Clum was interested, barely touching his coffee. After he had heard enough, Clum got up and called to his men, who were outside having a drink of Valley Tan with the hostlers while their employers were engaged in conversation.

As he mounted up, Clum told Greenfield that he wanted to stop Gwen before it was too late, because the Indians were ranging far and wide. He said they surely knew nothing about it and were in great danger.

"Well, if you try to catch 'em goin' over the new bridge, Mr. Clum, you'll be clean outa luck!" Greenfield said quickly, and Clum hesitated. "They're goin' farther down, over the old cutoff, headin' for the sandstone arch . . . you remember, the one folks used to use before it started fallin' to pieces a couple years back—"

Clum knew the arch. He roughly ordered the two hard-looking men with him to mount up, and they galloped off in the direction Gwen's party had taken. Greenfield watched them go, wondering at what a danged busy place this country was becoming. Tourists all summer long, and now, within the same hour, Jess Clum and Tom Quinn's daughter coming and going like there was no tomorrow. Horace Greenfield shook his head and yawned as he went back inside his stage station. Times sure were changing, and they were changing too fast for him, that was a fact!

By evening, Gwen and her friends had made thirty miles, all easy and comfortable, over the flats. They had forded the river without mishap, and with an hour of light to spare, they stopped for the night in a grassy meadow at the base of the Madison Range. The country became steeper here, and the road would divide in another mile. The south cutoff swung to the right around a mountain spur that stuck out into the valley, while the main road bore up and over the north side of the spur, then across the gorge at the new wooden bridge. Their route on the south cutoff would hug the foot of the mountain spur before bending eastward up a long canyon. The road would then rise steadily four or five hundred feet until they were high above the gorge that sliced through the mountain spur, separating it from the Madison Range. There— about eight miles south of the wooden bridge, where the Indians would be waiting if they intended to ambush the stage—they would find the sandstone arch.

Through his binoculars, Jordan had kept in sight the brave, who was following at a distance of a mile or so. The Indian probably did not know they had seen him. It would be better to wait until morning before taking the south cutoff; that way, the scout would have less time to alert his people to change their plans.

Camp that night was again uneasy for Jordan, but this time he would not have to bear the burden of watchfulness alone. Gwen and Meeker both took their turns at guard—the system was two hours on for each, with Jordan taking the first and last watches. During her guard tour, Gwen felt very lonely, even with Jordan asleep not far away. She stayed a little out of the firelight, as Jordan had suggested. "It's better they don't . . . ah . . . get a . . . ah . . . well, frankly, it's harder for them to get a good shot at you if they can't see you well, and that's all there is to it. So we'll sleep by the fire while you look and listen from over there in the dark when you're on guard. It's colder there, so take an extra blanket, and maybe Misty'll keep you company. But don't let yourself go to—"

"I won't go to sleep! Don't worry!"

But her watch was the third, and she felt incredibly weary when Amos woke her to take it. After sitting in the box of the bouncing coach all day, Gwen was exhausted. The four hours of rest she had taken seemed no more than a wink when

Meeker shook her. Now, huddled back from the fire and shivering in the blankets, she wished this night would end, begged it would end soon and everything be all right.

It was a night of timber wolves howling up the canyon, of yapping coyotes, and of eerie night noises that set her nerves on edge. It was cold and windy, with a steady breeze blowing down the valley, sweeping through their camp and chilling them. It whipped the fire to a white glow and sucked away the heat.

Once or twice, Gwen's head nodded, and when she snapped awake, her heart jumped. Each time, she wondered how long she had been sleeping. She felt inadequate, tired, and useless at those moments, angry with herself that she could not even take a two-hour watch without dozing off.

What was that? A horrible squeal burst from a thicket nearby. Gwen sprang up and aimed the Winchester. Something thrashed in the bushes, then skittered across a little clearing and wound up in other brush, giving a strange wailing whimper, then a thumping, as of something kicking the ground and sagebrush. Her heart thundering, Gwen moved slowly toward the sound—

"Come back."

She whirled at the voice, and Jordan knocked away the muzzle of the rifle, his face dark in the shadows of the fire, eyes gleaming. She began to tell him about the noise, but he simply put his arm around her shoulders and led her to the fire. "It's a rattler huntin' rabbits," he said. "I've heard the sound of a jackrabbit kickin' his last many a time. That's what you heard."

They sat down at the fire, and Jordan took the rifle from her. He felt her hands, which were still trembling. "You're cold," he said, and set about building up a blaze with dry sagebrush sticks and a thick cottonwood branch. "This'll do you—"

"But you shouldn't be awake yet," she protested. "Or haven't you trusted me enough to sleep?"

At her comment, he nodded toward Meeker, asleep in his blankets. "Amos trusts you well enough, I see." He looked at her and said simply, "So do I. I slept, and you forgot to wake me. Look at the sky."

Sure enough, the first light was mingling with the dark blue, already dimming the glitter of the eastern stars. She had missed waking Jordan by nearly two hours!

"Maybe I trusted you too much," he said. "But I did get a good rest." All the while, he was filling the pot from a canteen and readying coffee to brew.

Gwen said, "I'm sorry, Grant. I hope I didn't sleep too much."

"You don't look like you did," he said, setting the pot on the side of the blazing fire. "You look tired. You'll have to get some sleep inside the coach today."

Gwen felt at her face, wondering if she really looked so weary, so untidy. But Jordan interrupted her by saying, "But for someone who needs rest, you look mighty fine to me." He was smiling again, that same disarming, open way that appealed so to her, and she could not help smiling back, feeling a bit self-conscious.

"You still love me?" he asked, and Gwen's head came up quickly, but she did not reply.

She rubbed her hands together and held them out to the heat. She did not know whether to be annoyed or amused. As she thought for an answer, he smiled again. But this time she did not smile back—not because she was angry at his teasing but because she did not know exactly the right thing to say.

"Just joshin'," he said lamely, and glanced up at her as he took food out of a sack for breakfast.

"I figured that," Gwen replied. "That's why I won't answer your question."

Meeker coughed and stirred in his blankets, mumbling to himself and then sniffing. "Coffee brewin'." He grunted and sat up, pulling the blanket over his shoulders. "Ah, now that's a nice sight," he said, rubbing his eyes and yawning. "Coffee brewin' on the fire, cook fixin' vittles, and the lady of the house lookin' fit to horsewhip the cook."

They were off before the sun peeked over the mountains. For some reason, Jordan no longer felt they were being watched, though he often scanned the ridges on their left. They turned up the canyon on the old road, but still he saw nothing on the heights now on both sides of them. Perhaps the scout had already gone to fetch his war party.

Soon the road was rapidly rising, and it began to lead over the crown of the ridge. When the top of the ridge sharpened, the road came closer to the brink of a steep slope that fell away on the left, far down into a ravine. After another hour, the ridge soared above them on the right, and the road hugged a wall of rock. In places, the trail was no more than ten feet wide, here and there washed out, and it took all Meeker's skill to guide the stage safely over the bad spots. Many times, the iron wheel rims slid a little when the stage took a turn, and they sent sparks flying. Meeker went very slowly here, less than a mile an hour at best. Jordan was behind, leading the string of horses because they would only throw the stage off balance if they were tethered to it on this trail.

At first, Meeker had spoken to Gwen from time to time, but now he was all business and said nothing. As she sat in the jouncing driver's box, trying not to look down at the dizzying drop on her left, Gwen hung on for dear life, sure more than once that the coach was about to spill and throw them over the cliff to their deaths.

Meeker and his team picked their way up the trail, moving steadily, carefully. He was fighting an old road in perilous condition. At narrow places, where the rocks had sunk and slid away, Meeker spoke to the horses, calming them and telling them they were the best team in the Rocky Mountains. Then the coach would tip, leaning far over to the left until Gwen had to press against Meeker and bolster herself with her boots against the side rail to keep from sliding off. She was hypnotized, watching the litter of sand and boulders the wheels sent crashing down the side of the ridge.

But whenever they seemed about to heel over, Meeker brought the lurching stage upright again, and on they went, slowly, up and up. When the road led steeply downward, he played the foot brake and the horses to keep the heavily loaded coach from running away and knocking the animals off their feet. If Gwen had known fear before, the anxiety that gripped her now made all but the worst terrors pale in comparison.

After two hours of aching, agonizing toil, the stage climbed off the cliff face and rose over the crown of the ridge. Suddenly, it was high, wide-open plateau country, and there was bunch grass, silver-gray sagebrush, and a few hardy spruce trees. It was all blue sky and magnificent with the mountains looming so close; but no water was in sight. Meeker was troubled by that because his horses were tired and hot.

"We'll have to rest 'em soon. I want to give 'em a chance to recover from that climb before we make for the arch. The bridge is about half an hour away, I'd say, and I want to come at it with a team that's rested and not so nervous as it is now. Fact, I'd like to git a bit fresher myself after that last stretch." Gwen took a handkerchief and mopped sweat from his brow. "I thought I'd seen some squeezes in my stagin' days, but this was the squeezin'est."

Gwen was surprised to hear that, for she had thought Amos was so cool all the way and told him so. He smiled and shook his head, about to speak when suddenly shots went off behind them, and he was jolted forward, blood showing on his right shoulder. Gwen grabbed him and shouted his name, pulling him back as the team yanked ahead. Meeker gritted his teeth and steadied the lunging, frightened horses. He glanced at his wound, then urged the team into a fast gallop over the plateau.

Jordan, with the horses strung out behind him, came charging alongside, shouting, "Make for the bridge!"

"I am! I am!" Meeker shouted back.

Gwen wanted to call to Jordan and tell him that Amos was hit, but Jordan slowed, letting the coach pull ahead of him, and he drew out his revolver, half turning in the saddle to confront their attackers.

Chapter 10

The coach bounced and hurtled through the sagebrush, Meeker struggling to control the team. Gwen had her left hand gripping him by the front of his jacket, the other hooked over the back of the seat, holding on for both of them. Despite his wound, Amos seemed determined, strong, as he drove, but Gwen saw the pain in his eyes. His shoulder was completely stained red with blood, but he told her he was all right when she shouted to him over the pounding of the hooves and rattling of the coach. Then he looked her in the eye and said, "Get the dynamite."

She didn't hesitate, but reached inside his jacket and took out all three sticks. He told her the matches were in his shirt front, and she got them. Amos pushed the team hard, heading for a rise a mile or more ahead. Gwen could see the sandstone bridge there, reddish and orange-yellow, as it rose a little higher than the plateau and reached across the gorge that they knew was there but could not see yet. Gwen guessed Amos would slow down as he came to the arch—he would have to for fear of missing it and plunging over the brink.

Jordan rode behind them, about twenty yards from the coach. The Indians were another fifty yards farther back but closing the gap fast, taking long-range shots, but Jordan did not waste lead by returning their fire. He saw there were eight of them, all well mounted. If Amos misjudged his approach to the crossing, the stage would be cornered against the brink of the gorge, and they would have to shoot it out, as Gwen had done on the Beaverhead and likely with the same fatal results.

Meeker's dynamite could scare them off, but first, Jordan had another plan. He would release all the tethered packhorses and saddle mounts, and the horse-hungry braves would break off pursuit as sure as night follows day. It was still a good half mile of rugged ground to the sandstone bridge—and the dangers of the crumbling bridge would not stop the Indians, who were reckless horsemen and would cross it if the stage did. He galloped on, not pushing his horse hard, seeing at last that the Indians were near enough to make his move. He holstered his pistol.

Now! Jordan loosed the tether from his saddle horn, whipped off his hat, and pulled up the Appaloosa, whooping and waving at the confused horses. The animals veered off, turning to the right, and Jordan spun his own gelding and spurred away again.

But the bullets flew thickly. Jordan's gamble had cut too close to the line. Guns went off close behind him. To an Indian, lifting a scalp meant more than stealing a horse, and Jordan had made his own scalp suddenly seem easy to lift. He felt the whizz of lead, and he lay low on the Appaloosa, urging him on. Then the horse began to glide, like a great bird soaring close to the ground. Jordan spoke to it, and the gelding stretched his legs, the world speeding by faster and faster until he caught up to the thundering stagecoach and rode alongside. The arch was up ahead, now less than a hundred yards away. He glanced back and saw the Indians still coming on. They had not gone after the horses. Jordan drew his Colt and looked up at Meeker and Gwen. Meeker was shouting to him to ride ahead, motioning that he should go first over the bridge.

Jordan hesitated, reluctant to make a break for it when the slower stage might be caught. Then he saw the dynamite in Gwen's hands as she huddled against the seat with her back to the wind, trying to strike a match. He looked over his shoulder at three braves only thirty yards behind, firing pistols at the coach. Gwen was too good a target up there! He wanted to fight them off, but he knew what had to be done, and he drove his horse ahead, darting in front of the stage and charging onto the arch.

Immediately, Jordan saw that Greenfield's warning was accurate. The sandstone had worn and weathered away until just a foot's thickness remained in some places. The Appaloosa pounded over the bridge, which was about twelve feet wide and a hundred long. Dust rose, and fine silt cascaded over the side as the Appaloosa's hooves struck down. Then he saw, five hundred feet below, the thin ribbon of a stream glittering in the sunlight that slanted down into the chasm. It was a long, long way down. Jordan looked back to see the stage approach the bridge, horses foaming, dust flying, Indians right behind it now. Meeker had not slowed. He had to drive perfectly straight, or he would go over the edge. On the far side, Jordan jerked the horse around, gun in hand, ready to cover the stage. The arch was narrow!

Up in the box, Gwen's eyes were wide, fixed on the hissing fuse that had burned almost to the dynamite stick. Meeker was watching out of the corner of his eye, while the rest of his attention was on crossing the narrow span dead center. This was it! The horses thundered onto the natural bridge. The coach swayed, and Meeker had to control the frightened team. A lesser man would have lost it all. Then he yelled "Now!" and Gwen hurled the dynamite straight back over the coach. The stick hit the ground and bounced once almost under the feet of the first Indian, and with an ear-splitting boom, it exploded, bursting into flame, smoke, and dust, obliterating all view of the other end of the arch.

Jordan's horse reared in terror, and he fought the animal down, spinning as the stage barreled past at the same instant. He steadied the horse, ready for the first Indian to break through the cloud of dust. But there was none.

Even before the cloud blew away, Jordan knew no attackers would be coming after them this way, for the bridge was gone, its debris plummeting down into the gorge with two Indians and their horses. The dynamite had blown a fifteen-foot gap in the arch. A brave rider on a good horse could leap it if he had to, but Jordan doubted any Indian would take the risk.

Without looking back across the chasm, Jordan sent the gelding galloping along the road after the stagecoach, which had already disappeared down the trace into the thick stands of fir trees that covered this side of the mountain. He found the coach a quarter of a mile through the woods. Meeker had stopped in a broad, sunny clearing strewn with boulders, where a small stream ran into a pond. After the fury of the fight, it was like a dream in this peaceful spot, thought Jordan, feeling relief now that the danger was passed. He rode up to the stage, where the team was lathered and blowing. Inside the compartment, Misty whined, but he could not get out because the cargo had shifted in the flight and had sealed off the doors and windows. Jordan was about to announce their victory, but he saw Meeker lying back in the box and Gwen bent over him, tearing at his shirt.

Jordan leaped from his horse and sprang up to the old man's side. The bullet had hit Amos high on the shoulder, not a mortal wound if they took care of it soon but a painful one. It was a wonder he had been able to drive at all.

Gwen knew where she was by the lay of the land and the position of a few familiar peaks. They would hit the main road to the mine in a couple of miles or so. From there, by coach, it was about an hour to the mine.

They carried Meeker down to the ground and laid him in the grass by the stream. There they washed and bathed the wound, glad to see the bullet had passed through, though it had made a wicked, ragged exit and it was difficult to stop the flow of blood. Gwen said there was a man with some medical knowledge at the mining camp, and he could care for Meeker. They ripped up a shirt taken from Jordan's pack, which was stowed on top of the stage, and bound Amos as best they could. All the while, Misty whined, but they had to go on immediately, and there was no point letting the dog out yet. Suddenly, Misty began to bark.

Jordan went for his revolver and spun around. But there was nothing to be seen, only the pines hissing in the breeze. The mountains all around were silent, but Jordan felt that same sensation that had troubled him since they first came out of the Ruby Range: He was sure they were being watched.

Beside him, Meeker tried to sit up, saying, "I feel it, too. Somethin' in my bones says we ain't alone here."

Gwen, kneeling at the old man's side, searched the woods for some sign of what it was that made the men uneasy, but she saw nothing. She did not feel as restless as they, yet she knew their intuition was not to be taken lightly.

Oh, how she wished this trip were done! As close as they were to their goal, Gwen found it difficult to believe that they were really almost finished, that the money and explosives would be in her father's hands before the day was out. Somehow the thrill was not there as she once thought it would be. Somehow she had lost the urgent drive that had sent her out to Denver weeks ago. It was all very strange to Gwen, but as she knelt there—with Amos hurt and bleeding in her arms and Grant Jordan peering out at this lovely mountain wilderness with his pistol ready for danger—this whole adventure seemed to be a dream, as if in a distant haze, that would vanish if suddenly she awoke.

Then Jordan turned to her, and the dreamy sensation evaporated. His face was cold and hard, like a professional mountain man who had no patience for sentiment or emotion of any sort in time of trouble.

He said, "Let's go, then. But all of us got to keep watch every step from now on. We're through this far, but there's someone out there, an' whoever it is don't want to be seen. That makes me careful. Gwen, you ride alongside the coach. Amos'll ride up top, an' I'll drive. . . ."

Meeker spoke decisively. "Ever handled two span before, boy?"

Jordan shook his head. "But it's not far, an' I reckon this is a good time to learn."

Meeker cackled a little, summoned inner strength, and got to his feet despite Gwen's protests that he should be careful. "This ain't a good time to learn, boy," Meeker said, his jaw working against the pain from his shoulder, which still bled some. "If we do git hit again, we'll need a driver, not a guide."

Meeker walked unsteadily back to the coach, where Misty was barking. Jordan and Gwen watched him go, neither about to argue, because they knew he was right. They helped him get up into the box, and gritting his teeth, Meeker took the leathers in his hands. Gwen went up beside him again, though she knew it was a dangerous place to be. She now felt the same chilling sense that they were being watched, but even if she was a good target in the box, she knew she had to be close to Amos in case the loss of blood weakened him too much.

Without further conversation, Meeker started the team again, and Jordan mounted up to follow. They rode through sunny forest, up a gently rising trail of loose drift and scrubby grass. Even after they reached the main road and turned onto it for the last four miles to the Quinn mine, Grant Jordan was anxious, alert for another ambush—an ambush that would be easy to lay in this wild and beautiful country. As he rode, Jordan felt a gloomy foreboding that there would be more killing before he was through here. Again, he sensed an inner restlessness to travel north. The air was crisp and cool in bright sunlight at this high altitude, and every day he delayed in setting out for the plains meant one day closer to snow, one day closer to not getting away in time for the best hunting, when the buffalo hides were their thickest and game was still heavy from summer feeding.

When they swung around a cliff face that towered over a powerful river rushing by on the right, a cluster of log cabins appeared at the side of the river bank, smoke rising blue and faint in the sunshine-perfect autumn day. This was the Quinn mining camp.

Gwen stood up in the driver's box and gave a long, rising whoop that echoed up and down the river canyon, her voice bounding off the forested mountains that rose on every side. She turned to Jordan, her face alight with joy, and blew him a kiss. He smiled back at her. It was good, he thought, very good, that Gwen had succeeded. She had done all she had set out to do, and now it was up to her father to break through to the gold vein. Jordan looked at the mining camp, busy with men coming to meet them, then he glanced up at Gwen again. She was still gazing at him, but the smile had gone from her face and the light from her eyes as she watched him.

Then a shout came from down the cabins, and out of the crowd of miners came a big man wearing a battered old hat and hobbling along as fast as he could.

"Pa!" Gwen shrieked, and she jumped down to the ground before Meeker had pulled the team to a halt. She ran into Tom Quinn's arms, and Jordan saw the resemblance between father and daughter. Like her, he had fair hair. His face was ruddy, and his eyes were confident and self-assured—like his daughter's. But Jordan saw something else there, something drawn and taut, drained and utterly weary. The strain of the past months showed on Tom Quinn, yet Jordan noticed an inner strength that seemed to be surging as the miner drew Gwen close, hugging her without either of them speaking.

Then Quinn held the girl at arm's length and waited for her to speak. His eyes were full of pride and love at first, and when she said softly, "I brought the money, Papa . . ." Quinn shouted with joy and cried to the miners gathering around:

"You hear that, boys! We did it! The payroll's here! We did it!"

He swung Gwen around and laughed as the camp broke into a clamor of cheering and delight. The street of the little hamlet bustled with a score of men slapping each other on the back and shaking hands. Through the chatter and shouting, Tom Quinn asked Gwen, "Caleb and Silas! Where are they?"

It was then that Quinn realized his daughter was not filled with the same happiness that had swept him and the camp. "Hey, girl, you hear me? Where's your cousins?"

Before she could answer, her father glanced up at the stage and recognized Amos Meeker. Again, he roared with delight and shouted for the man to come down and be welcome. But once more Quinn was confused by the unexpectedly grave look on another face that should be happy.

"Well . . . what in tarnation . . . I say what's goin' on with you all? I seen happier folk at a fune—"

He cut off, and Gwen suddenly came into his arms. It began to come clear to him. Gwen was sobbing against his shoulder, and Quinn found himself struggling to ask the very question that had rolled so easily from him a moment before.

In a hoarse voice that was almost drowned out by the tumult of the celebrating miners, he asked, "Where's your cousins?"

Gwen pulled away, saying Amos needed medical help quickly. As two miners helped Amos down from the box, she made a brief introduction of Grant Jordan, who handed her the satchel with the payroll, then turned away to the old-timer. Tom Quinn saw his old friend's wound, and his eyes darkened.

Gwen watched Jordan let Misty out of the stage and walk off at Meeker's side. With the hound trailing, the two of them passed through the crowd of curious miners, all hushed now by the sight of blood.

"Amos and Grant Jordan saved my life," she said in a voice that seemed to her as though someone else were speaking. "If it wasn't for them . . ."

Her father's hand was on her shoulder. Again, he asked, "Where's Silas and Caleb?"

She sighed and without speaking led her father to his cabin, the money satchel slung over her shoulder. Meanwhile, at Quinn's orders, some miners began to unload the stagecoach.

Both Gwen and her father were quiet as they entered the cabin. Tom Quinn closed the door, standing with arms folded, waiting for Gwen to begin. Suddenly, it was as if all the misery, all the strain and anguish she had been through, flooded from her in that moment. She fell into her father's arms, sobbing and sobbing until, at last, he sat her down at the table and she told him everything.

After he had listened, Quinn sat beside his daughter and thought in silence for a while. His own eyes showed a hint of tears, for the boys had meant much to him. Even his daughter's success could not allay his sadness, and it was some time before either spoke again.

"I'd like to talk to this Jordan," Quinn said eventually. "It seems I owe him and old Amos."

They pulled themselves together and went outside. The mining camp was now a bustle of excitement—more excitement, said Quinn, than he'd seen in a year. As they walked among the cabins, Quinn called to his men and told them they would be paid that afternoon. Before night, he said, plans would be made for drilling holes for dynamite charges to be placed in the quartz rock down in the mine.

"We'll blast first thing in the morning," Quinn told the eager men who gathered around to hear him. "Then we'll strike what you've all been waiting for, and your shares in this will make you the richest hard-rock gold diggers in the Rockies."

The miners whooped and cheered him, slapping each other on the back, a few tossing hats into the air. Suddenly, the mood in the camp was confident, exuberant. Gwen saw that same mood come over her father as he strode among his men, giving orders and organizing this new stage in the enterprise. Only one thing dulled the camp's celebration, and that was the news of Silas and Caleb Quinn, both of whom had been well liked.

Preparations for the next day's blasting went ahead, and

Gwen Quinn was glad to see her father so decisive and self-assured—as he had not been for so many years. At first, she tried not to think of what the impending triumph had cost in blood and sorrow, but hard as she tried, she could not avoid those thoughts. Was it all really worth it, she wondered. For herself, striking it rich no longer held any special excitement. She had lived her life as a bulwark for her father, and now her world was changing, almost overnight, because wealth and professional success, his life's ambition, would be realized now. But as Gwen watched the bustle of the camp, it seemed she was sleepwalking. After what she had come through, the thrill the miners felt did not touch her the way it did them, and it actually repelled her because of the price that had been paid.

And so, after introducing Jordan to her father and leaving the two of them to talk, Gwen found herself wandering away from the hamlet, walking aimlessly through groves of pine and hemlock until she sat at the edge of the surging river that drove through the canyon. With the rush of water drowning out all else, Gwen let her mind rest, let it open and drink in the sunshine, as though it were a room that had been left darkened for much too long. Her head was tilted back, and her face bathed in warm sunlight, soothing and relaxing. The only reality was the warmth and the sound of the river rushing past.

Then she thought of where that river went, how it flowed through the canyons and down into the deep gorge under the sandstone arch that she had blown to smithereens—blown up along with two human beings. . . . That thought set her mind whirling again, and she opened her eyes, staring without seeing at the cascade of mountain water roaring past. In her thoughts, she recalled again the long, long journey to raise the money, the killing at the Beaverhead, the terror of being attacked . . . and the awful loss.

She shook her head to clear it and bit her lip to stop the trembling. It took all her power of will to return to the present moment—a moment that should be the prelude to triumph. . . . Then Grant Jordan entered her thoughts, and images of him ran through her mind. She saw him riding alongside the stage, grinning up at her in that way she liked so. Then he was fighting Jess Clum, and she was amazed by his strength. Her last vision of him was as the shadowy blur that rode out of the darkness on that first night and lifted her to safety.

All so romantic, she thought, and that made her smile a little. She tossed a pebble into the foaming water, and it vanished without the slightest ripple. *Like that, that's how he'll go.* But not quite without leaving a trace. No, he had touched her in a way she would never forget. She wondered just how she had touched him or whether she had touched him at all. She picked up another stone and threw it far into the river. Gazing, hardly thinking, Gwen once more let the sound of the water silence her mind.

Then a huge stone plunged into the river close by, splashing her, and she jumped back. Grant Jordan laughed and looked down at her, his hands on hips. She leaned back on her elbows and smiled at him.

"You're always there when least expected," she said as he sat beside her.

Jordan stared at her a moment, then turned to the river before saying, "You weren't expected, either."

They looked at each other, their eyes speaking for them. For a little while, they stayed that way, neither saying a word, yet both aware of the bond that had grown between them. Jordan looked away first, picking up a pebble and tossing it lightly in his hand.

"I'm going today," he said, gazing across the river.

Gwen did not reply. She had expected this, though perhaps not quite so soon. After a moment, she said, "Won't you stay until morning? I'd like you to tell me about the country you're going to."

He took his hat off and went to the bank of the stream. "It's flat," he said, lying on his stomach and filling the hat with cold water. He knelt and sloshed some on his face.

"That's all?" Gwen asked. "Just flat? You like flat country?"

He nodded. "I do. I like high country, too." He looked around the canyon and nodded. "Guess I like this country better than most I've seen."

"Then stay till tomorrow and enjoy it for at least this afternoon."

They looked at each other again, the way they had a moment before. Then he smiled a little and said, "I'll do that." He sat down near her and plucked a blade of grass to chew on. "You know it's not so much a country that I like or don't, it's the people there. And I like the people here. Your pa's a fine man. I understand why you ran the risks you did to help him. He's worth it, and he's worth havin' a daughter like you."

They sat there all afternoon, talking, listening to the river, watching an eagle soar around its eyrie high above. They knew this would be their last day together; neither wanted that sun to drop behind the cliffs, and when it did, neither wanted to make that slow walk back to the mining camp. They hardly talked at all then, strolling side by side in the chilly shade along the river. There was not much to say. There was too much to say. She could not ask him to stay, and he would not ask her to leave.

As they reached camp, walking with their heads down, seeing no more than the ground at their feet, Tom Quinn

stood at his cabin door, arms folded, watching them. For all
his hard times and difficulties, Quinn had seen enough of the
good side of life to know what was happening between these
two young people. He was a father who loved his daughter,
so his own thoughts were confused just then, but he wanted
Gwen to be happy; that was sure. That was most important.
He wondered whether she might miss a chance to find that
happiness if she let Grant Jordan leave too easily.

When they came near, he called to Jordan, asking him to
stay for dinner. The hunter was grateful for Tom Quinn's
invitation. Not only did he genuinely like the miner, but he
wanted to spend a little more time with Gwen before going
off to sleep in a spare bunk in a cabin above the camp. Amos
Meeker was there also, his arm bound up in a sling. Meeker
was drawn and pale, even in the light of candles and a roaring
fireplace, but he had been treated skillfully by the camp's
amateur doctor, and he would recover in a few weeks. At
Meeker's feet, near the fire, lay Misty, who raised his eye-
lids, but nothing more, as Gwen and Jordan came in.

They ate a simple, filling meal around the pine kitchen
table, talking of mining prospects and of the hunting up
north. As evening drew on, Quinn made it clear to Jordan
that he thought the future here was brighter than that of a
drifting professional hunter.

"Might be so," Jordan said, settling back with a briar pipe
and stretching out his legs toward the fire. "But a man does
what he knows, and this one knows huntin'. If you're makin'
an offer of a job, Tom, I'm much obliged, but I'm no minin'
man."

Quinn filled his own pipe and said, "I'm making the offer.
You could learn whatever you need to know. But after we
strike the vein, it won't take long to make enough to hire
more miners; then a man with a share in this business could

take his profits and make any life he wants for himself. Just 'cause I've been a gold hunter all these years doesn't mean I want to stay one. No, sir. I aim to make my pile, then build a hotel back Denver way. Maybe get into politics a little. I was a member of the territorial legislature here, and a man can do a lot of good in government if he's honest! Now I figure you've earned a share in it when the gold comes, and you can do what you want when you get it.''

But Jordan declined politely, glancing at Gwen as he did so. She sat on a stool close to the fire, holding a hot cup of tea, staring into the flames.

"I guess men might call me a fool, Tom," Jordan said quietly. "But when the travelin' life gets into the blood, it stays a long time, maybe forever. It's not the same as gold fever, but it's somethin' like it, I'd say. Gold hunters got their eyes to the rivers and the rocks. I got my eye on the crest of the next hill.''

"Ever find it?" Meeker asked, also staring at the fire, which was the dominating light in the room. "Ever find what you was searchin' for, son?"

Jordan thought for a moment. Then, when he was about to speak, Gwen got up, put her cup on the table, and without looking at anyone, went outside and closed the door.

The three men sat silently, with the crackling of the fire the only sound. After a few moments, Quinn said, "The offer's open if you decide to come back, boy." Then he paused before adding, "Why don't you say good-bye to her?"

Jordan got up and knocked his pipe out against the hearthstone. Then he gathered his jacket and hat, bade farewell, shaking hands warmly and wishing Amos and Quinn luck, and went out into the cool night.

He closed the door behind him and searched the darkness for some sign of Gwen. The night sky was a cloud of stars, crystal clear and glittering. A mountain night was not as limitless as night over the plains, but it was sharp and filled with a glory that only high country possesses. Jordan inhaled deeply, and the brisk air felt pure. Then he heard the sound, faint and uncertain, as of someone trying to catch a breath near the corner of the cabin, in darker shadows. Jordan knew it was Gwen. He went to her, and she heard him coming. She fought back tears and tried to wipe them away. As he reached her, she turned to face him, feeling foolish and childish and embarrassed all at once. He came close and took her by the shoulders. Gwen felt the tears insisting again, and this time she could not hold them back. Then she was against him, her forehead on his chest, her arms held close against her body. His arms went around her, and he kissed her hair. They stood like that for a long time until Jordan spoke.

"You know, this is the first time I ever even thought I'd like to stay someplace."

She sniffed and put her arms around his waist, leaning against him.

He said, "Must be the people here," and pushed her back a little so he could look at her face in the starlight. "Don't cry. It doesn't suit you."

She gave a little laugh and put her forehead against his chest once more. She sighed, and he took a deep breath. Then she said, "I do love you."

He kissed her forehead and lifted her chin to look at her closely. "I love you, too. And that's why I have to go . . . I can't make you happy . . . the kind of man I am—"

"Do you have to be that way, then?" she asked quickly. "You haven't always been a drifter! You once knew what it was to have a home! Why can't you try here . . . if . . . if you mean what you say! If you do . . . really love me!"

He touched her lips with his fingers and caressed her

cheek. She took his hand, and he drew her to him and kissed her gently, but carefully, without letting himself go. Gwen trembled and moved back, her head down, trying to think of the right words, but none came.

"Good-bye," he said, and she looked up quickly. He released her hand and vanished into darkness just as he had come, as if perhaps he had really never been there at all.

Chapter 11

The sun was peeking over the eastern cliffs when Jordan mounted the Appaloosa and led a packhorse Quinn had given him out the canyon on a trail that went around the mining camp. He took that trail, not wanting to encounter Gwen again. He had lain awake much of the night thinking about her, wrestling with his emotions, and finally seeing the sun come up with his mind still turning over and over.

But now he was on his way. As he had told Tom Quinn last night, a hunter is drawn by the season's best hunting grounds, and this was the time of year to head north. No matter what fortune might be his if he stayed at the mining camp, Grant Jordan was not sure he could be tied to one woman, even if that woman was Gwen Quinn. He did not want her to suffer if he tried and found that life impossible. So he moved on along the narrow path in the evergreens above the camp, looking down at the hamlet lying in bright sunshine. He saw the men walking up to work at the mine in the side of the mountain just below the trail. Already he had heard several deep blasts from the mine. Quinn's first shift had begun dynamiting early, as planned.

After passing the camp, Jordan took the path down to the main road, and he had almost come out of the trees when he heard the sound of horses rapidly approaching. He pulled up, keeping to the underbrush. Five men came into sight, riding hard along the canyon road toward the camp from the same direction as Jordan's party had come the day before. He was relieved to see they were civilians, not soldiers looking for him. The men were all dressed roughly except for the one leading them, who was riding a chestnut. He was natty in a black suit, waistcoat, and beige derby. Then Jordan recognized him: Jess Clum! What was Clum doing here? Was he working for Rutledge?

Jordan was concealed in the trees as Clum and his followers rode past. He watched them ride down the trail and stop in front of Tom Quinn's cabin. Quinn came out to meet Clum, and the two men entered the cabin, closing the door. Jordan did not like the looks of the hard cases with Clum, and he decided he ought to wait a bit before leaving.

Just then, a rustling in the bushes on his right caused him to spin, and the Colt was suddenly in his hand. Out came Kintara mounted on a roan. Jordan put up the pistol as the warrior motioned for him to follow. Kintara said nothing as, together, they took a path that ran parallel with the main trail, and Jordan followed the Indian's lead, keeping silent, moving at a walk through the woods.

Gwen was standing near her bedroom door, listening in dismay as Jess Clum told her father why he was there and whom he represented. Clum was leaning forward, hands flat on the table, while Quinn stood straight, arms folded, listening.

"Tom, you have to understand I'm doing this for your own good," Clum was saying. "No matter what difficulties you and I might have had in the past, I came here because we were partners once, and I figure you deserve the warning. You have to sell this mine, and sell it now, or you won't have a thing to sell come springtime.''

Quinn was silent, but his face showed he was restraining anger as he listened. In the background, they heard the blasting from the mine. Clum went on. ''Tom, you may have gold back in there, but you haven't the capital to develop it, and you never will. Now I've been asked by the Salt Lake City syndicate to—''

''You?'' Gwen broke in, stepping forward. ''You're with them?''

Clum put up his hand to still her. ''Miss Quinn, I hope that if I can't convince your father of what's right, at least you'll listen to reason. Yes, I'm with the syndicate, it's true, but I came here today as a friend, not as a representative of theirs. . . .''

Clum went on to say that the syndicate was willing to offer a fair price for the mine if Quinn sold out immediately. But as far as Gwen was concerned, the price he quoted was less than a third of what the mine was already worth, and she said so. That did not slow Clum, who declared that the syndicate was already taking legal steps to require Tom Quinn immediately to pay up all overdue installments on the mortgage they held on the mine. Its members would wait no longer to be paid, and Quinn was now under new pressure. The amount due, said Clum, came to nearly five thousand dollars. Gwen knew her father would be ruined if he had to turn over all that money immediately, and Clum echoed her thoughts when he said, ''Now I know the ten thousand your daughter raised is just enough to see you through a few months. But if you have to use half to pay off—''

''Wait a minute!'' Gwen cried, coming to her father's side.

"How do you know about that money? How . . . what business is it—"

Clum again put his hand up and looked down at the table as he said with exasperation, "Miss Quinn, surely you realize I know everyone in Virginia City, including the Wells Fargo agent and his good wife. . . . I have my ways. Surely you realize that your aiding the escape of a white renegade has lowered your reputation in the territory so that it was not difficult for me to learn whatever I wanted."

"What!"

"Of course," Clum said with a sneer, "the army never needs to know about your poor judgment if only Tom here will agree to sell—"

But before Clum could finish, Tom Quinn rushed around the table and yanked him by the shirtfront, hurling the man against a wall of the cabin, derby and cane flying. In the next moment, Clum was thrown out the door, and after him sailed the derby. Quinn strode out into the sunlight with the ebony cane in his hands and stood over Clum, who was winded and shaken. Clum's men, lounging by their horses a short distance away, came running when they saw their employer land on his back. But they stopped in their tracks as Gwen came out behind her father, her Winchester leveled at them.

Tom Quinn said in a calm, steady voice, "Go back to your friends. Tell them they'll get whatever I owe them. Show your face around here again and—"

Quinn snapped the cane in two and tossed it at Clum's feet.

Without replying, Clum lumbered to his horse, mounted up, and hurried away with his men. Gwen let out a long breath. She was surprised he had been run off so easily.

Amos Meeker joined them, still wearing a sling, a shotgun in the crook of his good arm. He had been concealed close by in case trouble started with Clum and his men. The three of them stood listening to the sound of the riders dwindling in the distance, then Meeker said, "They'll be back, Tom. There's more to this yet."

Quinn sighed and nodded. "We haven't seen the last of Jess Clum." He looked at his daughter. "I wish that Jordan fellow hadn't left us just yet . . . we might need him afore too long."

Gwen said nothing. Meeker hefted the shotgun inside his sling so his good arm was free and said, "I think I'll take a walk up the trail a ways, jest to make sure them varmints has cleared out."

"I'll go with you," Gwen said quickly, and the two of them left Quinn at the door of his cabin.

Just then, Grant Jordan was kneeling in thick bushes with Kintara at his side, watching a dozen men who were standing near a string of packhorses and ponies. The men passed a jug around, and each looked tougher than the last. Kintara whispered to Jordan that his people had been trailing this bunch for a few days, adding that they were bad medicine. Then he said, "Crow scouts follow your party, too, Jordan, to see horse soldiers don't catch you."

Then it came clear to Jordan that it was the Crows who had been watching over him since they left the Ruby Mountains, and it was their scouts he had seen in the distance from time to time. But when Kintara then told him that this group of whites had attacked his stagecoach, he was confused. Before he could ask Kintara to explain, they heard horses coming back down the trail from the mining camp. In a moment, Jess Clum appeared and yanked his chestnut to a stop, the others riding in just behind him, and he shouted loud enough so that Jordan could hear.

"All right, boys, go in! Do what I told you and make it look good. Nobody gets out! Nobody!"

Jordan was surprised by what he saw next, but he realized

quickly that he should have figured on this. The ruffians laughed among themselves as they dragged Indian gear from the packhorses, pulled on wigs and feathers, and streaked red and yellow war paint on their faces. Then they chose their ponies, throwing saddle blankets over them, and soon they looked the part of a Crow war band.

Clum was the only one of the seventeen who did not disguise himself. He sat his chestnut like a general readying his troops. Jordan glanced at Kintara, and each understood what was happening. Here were the real hostiles who had attacked Quinn's supply wagons and had killed Gwen's cousins on the Beaverhead! It was clear Clum had engineered the Indian massacre at Virginia City in the hopes of forcing the true Crows into hostilities, that way covering up his own murderous designs. Jordan still knew nothing of Clum's connection with the mining syndicate that wanted Quinn's gold mine, but Clum's motives did not matter at all just then. There was nothing Jordan could do alone to prevent an attack on the mining camp. They passed sign language, and Kintara stole away. Now it was up to Jordan to keep Clum from escaping.

He slipped back down the path and found his Appaloosa. He felt cold fear for Gwen's safety. If he captured Clum, perhaps he could force him to call off the attack. He spurred the horse ahead on the path and down onto the main road. Then he heard another rider approach. Too late, Jordan tried to pull his horse off the trail, but Clum saw him and reined in, drawing his revolver and firing. Jordan ducked, whipped out his Colt, and let fly. But Clum had already turned and vanished around a bend in the overgrown trail. Jordan sent his horse galloping after him.

A short distance from the camp, Gwen and Amos walked in silence along the road, in the shade of pines. There the world seemed to slumber out of sight of the sun. Insects buzzed, and a butterfly whisked around their legs. Gwen watched it flutter its erratic way and thought it looked so carefree that for a moment she envied it. Then Meeker stopped and took her by the arm, clutching so hard that it hurt. "Listen!" he whispered.

A drumming was in the air, and the woods began to fill up with the sound of many horses approaching, running hard.

"What is it?" Gwen began to ask, but Meeker jerked her off the trail, and they hid behind the trunk of a thick pine. The drumming grew louder, and Gwen's heart began to race with it. Then, from around a turn in the trail rode an Indian warrior, and another, and yet another. The riders pounded past, and fear clutched at Gwen as she realized her father's camp was about to be attacked. Another horseman whipped into sight, followed by more savage-faced Indians, several carrying flaming pitch-pine torches, until Gwen counted sixteen charging down the trail.

She wanted to jump up and open fire, but when she made a move, Meeker gripped her arm and held her back. His eyes were ablaze watching the riders thunder past.

When it was all clear, with a jerk of the head, he beckoned for her to follow, and they set off at a run toward the camp, about a hundred yards away. Then the shooting began, and Gwen wanted to shout, to scream a warning, but she knew that was a fool's move—that the only way they could help the camp was to come up from behind and surprise the attackers. But what good two more guns could do against so many, she did not know. Her mind whisked to a vision of Grant Jordan, but she forced it away, knowing there was no time now for that. They ran toward the sound of guns, and Gwen smelled smoke. At least one of the buildings had been set afire. She could hear horses screaming and the voices of men shouting, and her heart quickened as they neared the clearing where the mining hamlet lay. Meeker motioned for her to follow him into bushes at the edge of the trees.

Fear welled up in Gwen, and her mouth was dry as they worked their way the last yards toward the clearing. She almost cried out when she saw her father's cabin was ablaze. The bodies of two miners lay in the little street before the cabin, and the sound of gunfire was only sporadic. The attack had been a complete surprise, and the miners had been driven to cover with little chance to fight back.

Then she heard firing from her father's cabin, and she saw someone was still inside even though the roof was roaring in flame. The Indians were riding up and down the camp, firing into the windows and doors of cabins, throwing flaming brands onto wagons and buildings. There, in front of Quinn's cabin, was the stage, as yet untouched, and Gwen sensed Meeker was staring at it most of all. The Indians charged back and forth, shrieking and yelping savagely, in complete control of the hamlet except for her father's cabin. Between Gwen's and Meeker's position in the trees was a corral that held the stage horses, penned and terrified, racing about. Next came the street and the stagecoach in front of the cabin where Tom Quinn was fighting for his life.

The main body of miners was up at the mine, and there they were doomed once the Indians finished with the cabins and went up after them. There were few guns with the miners, who would surely be taken by complete surprise. Most of the men were below ground, blasting at the quartz, and they would not even hear the gunfire above ground until it was too late.

"We have to do something!" Gwen begged Amos.

Amos was thinking hard. Then he said quickly, "You get to the corral next time the Injuns ride to the other end of camp. Then I'll git yer pa out. Cover me, an' keep 'em busy! Keep 'em at the other end, hear? When I bring Tom out, you follow us back here, and we'll make a break for it into the woods; then we'll swing up to the mine and help the boys up there from goin' under without havin' a chance!''

The band of Indians rode down the camp street past Quinn's house, all of them low on their mounts, firing into his cabin as they passed. Then they wheeled their horses and came back the other way, all sixteen of them, pouring a rain of lead into the blazing building.

When the Indians charged away, turning their backs to Gwen and Amos, the two of them dashed into the open, Gwen darting for the corral fence and Meeker, his bad arm held tightly against his body, running across the street and into the cabin where they thought her father was. The Indians were wheeling fast. One of them saw Meeker's move and gave a whoop. The attackers came on again, fast and head-long, from less than a hundred yards away. Gwen opened up with her Winchester when they were half that distance away, and the first two Indians went down. A third had his mount shot out from underneath him, and he scrambled up behind another horseman. The party pulled up suddenly, surprised at this fierce counterattack, and they rode back to the other end of camp to plan their next move. Gwen reloaded and waited for Meeker to appear with her father.

Clum came into sight after a few hundred yards. Jordan's big Appaloosa was closing with every step. Clum glanced frantically over his shoulder and began to whip his chestnut, but it was no use, and he knew it. His was not the horse to outrun Jordan's gelding. A few minutes later, they were close to the fork that turned off toward the ruined natural bridge, and by now, Jordan was near enough to try a shot at his enemy.

The bullet nicked the rump of Clum's animal, and it panicked, lunging out of control and nearly unseating its rider.

Clum barely held on, but the chestnut had its head now, and when it came to the fork in the road, it swerved to the left, off the main road toward the ruined natural bridge. Now Jordan had his man! There was no escape for Clum with the deep gorge in front of him and Jordan coming on behind. Clum would soon be at bay, cornered, and he would be forced to turn and fight it out, face to face.

As they raced out of the pine-shrouded trail into a broad, sunny meadow, Jordan closed the gap to less than forty yards. It was another three hundred yards to the bridge now, and Jordan could see it through the dust, jutting up into space at its center, where the dynamite had shattered it. Jordan was ready for Clum to dismount at any minute and take cover. But Clum was not slowing his mount. Instead, he had brought it under control again and was heading straight for the bridge. Jordan realized his quarry was taking this one route of escape: He was about to jump the chasm, about to gamble his life on that fifteen-foot gap in the middle of the bridge. And if Jordan wanted to stay with him, he would have to do the same—as he knew he would, for this killer must not get away.

He drove his gelding closer, now only twenty yards back, and only a hundred yards from the bridge. Again he aimed and fired. Clum winced, just keeping his seat but holding on to his right leg, which showed a spurt of blood. Clum's horse hit the bridge, galloping along the narrow remains of the near side. Jordan was right behind, and he saw the chestnut abruptly leap. But Clum's wound was bad, and he was off balance when his horse went up. Like a rag doll, he jerked backward in the saddle and screamed in horror as he felt himself falling. Jordan yanked his Appaloosa to a skidding stop right at the brink of the chasm, and he fought to control his plunging horse as its hooves sent loose debris cascading over the edge.

On the other side of the gap, Clum's chestnut was still running, but its saddle was empty, its stirrups flapping wildly, and far below, the body of Jess Clum lay shattered and broken on the bank of the stream that surged through the bottom of the gorge.

Without hesitation, Jordan wheeled his lathered Appaloosa and sent him galloping back down the mine road, hoping desperately that he was not too late.

Gwen had little hope of lasting much longer. As she had expected, the fourteen Indians divided into two groups, nine dismounting and disappearing on her left into the trees and the other five racing down the street at a wild gallop. Gwen knelt by the rail fence and took aim. There was no way she could fight off both groups at once, but she would make her shots count against the ones she could see.

When the Indians reached the same position as before, she opened fire, rapidly pumping the entire magazine of fifteen bullets at them. Horses and riders went down in a cloud of dust, but three broke through, thundering right for her. She was out of ammunition, and she froze, watching the attackers bear down.

Then, like a bolt of lightning, Amos Meeker's shotgun and her father's pistol erupted from behind the stagecoach, and two Indians were demolished, blown out of their seats. The third ducked and charged Gwen, completely intent on her, swinging a tomahawk. She stood her ground, ready to brandish the empty rifle like a club.

The Indian came at her, and she barely managed to jump clear, smacking his horse on the neck with the rifle as she moved, making it rear. The warrior's tomahawk whisked past her face again and again. She came around with the butt of the rifle, swinging at the horse with all her might, but the

shock of striking the animal's chest jarred her as though she
had been struck herself, and she staggered, dropping the
weapon. The Indian leaped from his mount and lunged at her.
Gwen backed off quickly and stumbled, falling, and he was
on her, heavy and stinking. She fought with desperate strength,
but it was useless. The man was on top of her, his weight
bearing down, his hands pinning her arms, and his knees
digging at her legs. She realized he was not going to kill her
yet.

In the blur of frenzied struggle, Gwen saw what she thought
must have been madness: The Indian's eyes were blue! But
that was all she saw, and she struggled against him, every
writhing twist of her body dragging her strength away until,
finally—

The brave screamed and fell from her. His terrible weight
was gone! Her arms were free! All around was the roar of
gunfire and the savage whooping of many, many Indians.
She was stunned and numb, and she tried dizzily to sit up.
Horses were charging past her, and men were running. It
seemed there were a hundred Indians instead of just a few. In
the wild confusion, an Indian grabbed her arms and helped
her stand. He was tall and young, wearing a bright-red shirt.
Gwen's head ached, and she swayed on her feet, all the while
staring at this warrior, who was grinning at her, simply
grinning while the smoke and sounds of fighting came from
every side at once. Now the Indian was speaking. . . .
Gwen tried to focus on him, but she felt faint, and all she saw
was that red shirt. What was he saying? . . . *Kintara?* Was
that his? . . . Overcome by dizziness, Gwen fell. But she did
not hit the ground. Instead, she found herself in the arms of
Grant Jordan, whose face was close to hers, and he was
saying something. Over the roar of the battle, she could not
understand him. Yet it did not matter at all just then. She

murmured his name over and over and then let everything go. For the first time in her life, Gwen Quinn fainted.

A week later, just as the light began to filter into Alder Gulch, a sleepy sentry walking his post on the perimeter of the Virginia City cavalry camp was shocked alert. What he saw stunned him at first, then sent him shouting in fright through the camp: "Indians! Indians! Hundreds of 'em!"

He stumbled toward the commandant's tent, and out stepped Lieutenant Wilkinson in only his army trousers and undershirt. As men hurried out of their tents up and down the company street, the soldier tried to tell Lieutenant Wilkinson what he had seen. Wilkinson hurried into his boots and blouse, pushed his hat on, and trying to buckle on his saber as he went, followed the soldier. When he reached the sentry's post, Wilkinson's chin dropped, and the unbuckled saber fell to the ground. There, a thousand yards away on the crest of a hill, were three hundred Crow warriors, all mounted, all armed and apparently ready to sweep down into his flimsy camp.

Wilkinson shouted for Corporal Buchanan, standing nearby, to call out the Gatling gun crew, and then he began to give a babble of orders to whoever was at hand. All the while, he was clumsily, unsuccessfully trying to buckle on his scabbard. At last, when Wilkinson realized that Corporal Buchanan had not made a move to obey his orders, he screeched at him, but Buchanan simply put a finger to his lips and pointed up the hill at the Indians.

"I'd say, sir," Buchanan spoke soothingly, still pointing at the Indians, "that they don't intend comin' at us with a stagecoach in their front rank."

Wilkinson jerked around, eyes wide. Sure enough, set against the pink eastern dawn, was the outline of a stagecoach on the crest of the hill. Wilkinson stared, astonished and confused. Buchanan spoke again. "An' it looks like there's a flag o' truce there on that stagecoach, don't it, Lieutenant?" Buchanan tried not to smile, but he failed.

While the soldiers dressed and armed themselves, the Indians sat patiently on their horses. At Buchanan's quiet suggestion, Wilkinson refrained from limbering the Gatling gun to take it out as a threat to these warriors. A short while later, the stagecoach and two horsemen moved down the slope a hundred yards in front of the Indians and stopped, the truce flag fluttering on the coach.

Wilkinson fetched a white flag and took Corporal Buchanan along with him to carry it. They rode up the hill toward the Indians. Visibly shaking, Wilkinson drew rein in front of the coach, and he was surprised to see Amos Meeker in the driver's box, with Kintara sitting proudly at his side, Winchester over his knees like a shotgun messenger.

One of the horsemen was Grant Jordan, the other Gwen Quinn, and Wilkinson's confusion mounted. Not a word was spoken until Tom Quinn stuck his head out of the coach window and shouted, "We want to see that bug-tit Willie Rutledge, Lieutenant! I'll thank you to send him up here and tell him we got nothing to say to a pipsqueak like you!"

Wilkinson said, with difficulty, "Mr. Quinn, I have to inform you that I am in command of this camp now. . . . Ever since Captain Rutledge was . . . ah . . . was . . ." He struggled with the next word and finally spat it out. "Transferred!"

"To the Florida swamps," said Billy Buchanan with a gleeful face.

The others at the coach waited for Wilkinson to explain himself. He said glumly, "There was an army hearing just after the Crow . . . troubles . . . and it seems that Captain

Rutledge was not . . . ah . . . supported in his actions . . . and the high command deemed it fitting that he should have another posting in a less sensitive area—"

"Who spoke against him?" Quinn asked.

Wilkinson cleared his throat a moment before saying, "I . . . and the troopers of the command, Mr. Quinn." Then, while Jordan and his friends looked at one another, Wilkinson went on. "And now, Mr. Quinn, as you seem to be spokesman for this embassy, would you please tell me just what is going on?"

Quinn nodded and grinned. "Well, Lieutenant, what you see is a good piece of the Crow nation, come in to treat with the army once and for all. They came here under my protection, since I am a former representative to the territorial legislature. They trust me to plead their case—particularly since I made their chiefs full partners in my new gold strike in the Madisons. I guess now they'll have the wherewithal to hire a lawyer and get a formal hearing for the killing you and Rutledge did here a while back. . . ."

Wilkinson's face was pale as he listened to Quinn state the Indians' case and end with "Also, Mr. Grant Jordan, my partner in our new gold strike, intends to press his own complaint against the U.S. Army, Lieutenant, so if you'll turn yourself around and head down to your camp there, we'll follow to fill out the necessary papers, and I'll tell you a story about a friend of yours—Jess Clum, that is. It's a story you can think about while you're sportin' with the alligators yourself, you . . ."

But Wilkinson had heard enough. He yanked his horse around, and without waiting for Buchanan, galloped back to camp. Buchanan's face had a look of delight, and he told Jordan, "Lots happened here after you left, old hoss."

Jordan indicated the missing stripes on Buchanan's sleeve and said, "I can see that, Billy. I'm sorry—"

"Shucks," Buchanan said, shaking his head slowly, "I'll get 'em back soon enough, an' it was worth it to see Rutledge get his. Why this place was filled to bustin' with colonels and generals the like I ain't seen since the war, an' all of 'em itchin' to blame somebody for what Rutledge and Wilkinson did to the Crows. Well, Wilkinson took his chance and testified against Rutledge quick as a snake, and that opened the door for the troopers to speak up. Didn't take long as army hearings go, and Rutledge was on his way. Looks like Wilkinson'll be gone, too, once you all get yore hand in.

"An' you won't have to worry much, old hoss, 'cause the charges agin you was brought by Rutledge, an' it ain't likely anybody else'll want yore hide, not now that every army politician, Indian agent, and aspirin' vote getter for miles around is jumpin' on the bandwagon an' tryin' to be on the winnin' side of this mess—an' the winnin's side ain't Wilkinson's.

"I guess, old hoss, you'll be headin' north now, though it's some late in the season, I'd say." Buchanan looked closely at Gwen, sitting her horse close to Jordan, and he grinned. "If you do go north, Jordan, this child'd say you was a sorry excuse for a Reb!"

Jordan glanced at Gwen, dressed prettily in a riding jacket and dark skirt. She was even riding sidesaddle for the occasion. "You said you were set on havin' a sergeant major as the best man at the weddin', weren't you?" he asked her.

"I wouldn't object to a corporal," she replied, and gave Buchanan a glowing smile.

Buchanan stood up in his stirrups and let out a yahoo loud enough to startle the stage team, and Amos hauled the animals in before they could pull away. Then Buchanan whirled his horse and charged down the hill, the white flag he held snapping gaily. He gave a wild, drawn-out rebel yell that echoed up and down Alder Gulch, waking all of Virginia City and even setting old Misty to howling. Amos cackled and gave the team a word, and the stage rumbled on down the slope, with Tom Quinn beaming happily inside, Kintara stoic and grim up on top. Then came Gwen and Jordan, riding side by side, slowly now, as though they had all the time in the world together.

Coming in June 1983...

STAGECOACH STATION 6:

SANTA FE
by Hank Mitchum

On a blustery morning early in November 1867, a stagecoach leaves the railhead at Hays City, Kansas, for the four-and-a-half day run to Santa Fe. On board is Beth Hanlon, daughter of stage-line owner Tom Hanlon. She is on her way to be reunited both with her father—who has been seriously injured in a stage accident—and with her fiance, Frank Colby, general manager of the stage line.

Unbeknownst to Beth and the other passengers, someone else is making the run between Hays City and Santa Fe—but in the opposite direction. Frank Colby has been embezzling funds from the stage line and is now fleeing Tom Hanlon's wrath. Taking along what is left of the money, he intends to find Beth and convince her to marry him at once.

Caught, in a crossfire of emotions—and facing the dangers of Indians, desperados and savage mountain weather—Beth must rely on her own inner strength as she struggles to survive.

Read SANTA FE, on sale June 1983 wherever Bantam paperbacks are sold.